T0192903

THE Electro-Encephalo-Grapher Couldn't Cry

Other Titles in the Adam Quatrology

Adam's Big Bang
Return of the Horla
The Radio

THE Electro-Encephalo-Grapher Couldn't Cry

A Novel

BERNARD SUSSMAN

Bartleby Press
Washington • Baltimore

Published by:

Bartleby Press

PO Box 858
Savage, Maryland 20763
800-953-9929
www.BartlebythePublisher.com

Library of Congress Cataloging-in-Publication Data

Sussman, Bernard, 1926-2017
    `The electroencephalographer couldn't cry / Bernard Sussman.
        p.   cm.
    ISBN 978-0935437-52-2 (paperback)
    I. Title.
    PS3569.U796E4   1999   96-21294
    813'.54--dc20   CIP

Printed in the United States of America

For Claire, Pat and Bob

One

He reared up, suddenly awake and fearful. Still fully alive or slipping away? Frantic to know, he turned on to one elbow and drew quick breaths. They came, but not easily. Was the breathing quite deep enough? Inspiration seemed restricted, not full, not of the life supporting kind. Grabbing at his neck, he felt for a carotid pulse, "Please! God?" Yes, yes it was there for him. Hard to get, but only because it was racing! So his shallow breaths could not be just the final few gulps of air drawn in reflexly, like after a cardiac arrest. Somewhat reassured, he fell back again, not to sleep, but to observe with envy the easy normal breathing of the woman, his wife, whose respirations his own soon mimicked, as he permitted them to recede from his awareness.

Returned to life he was, but forced again by this rude reminder to contemplate the horror of being someday truly dead, the horror of oblivion, of death as reality, not some thing vague, remote, however guaranteed. He lay there, thinking of the prospect of dying as a genuine experience, a process to be felt, not something just theoretical. Heart no longer pounding, he wanted to sleep again, but thought it hardly safe to do so. Next time, it could happen.

Life, for him, had become no more nor less than death awaited, scarcely different from death itself. And everyone else was on death row too, for a vulgar or sinister reason, or for something else, eluding memory. He could not say he understood this, only that he had an odd sense of things having gone on this way a very long time, a trifle short of existence. His inclination, a bizarre one, was to hold both life itself and some other thing at fault, responsible. He wondered at times if his suspicions might constitute a flaw in an intended order of things and not be long tolerated if some mystery needed preserving.

The first inkling of death had come to him when he was a child of three in the garden of his father's aunt. He'd certainly had no reason at that uninformed age to grasp the awful implication of his newness. There could be no logic of relationships involving time behind a sensing, felt with infantile awe, that the sweet smelling, almost pitch black earth piled up loosely in that rose bed, was to him, as every other kind of dirt would always be, peculiarly ancient, perhaps even prehistoric. But more than that, he seemed to see in the broken, freshly spaded, aromatic ground; shadowy events, obscure indications, soundings of failed lives and times past, where anyone else, and certainly an untutored groping child, would just observe top soil, or the squirming of an occasional upended worm. He was even too entranced by his special visions to pay any notice at all to the bright and happily bursting plants his parents came to admire or sniff over, and for which his attention was ardently solicited by all of those old ones. "See the pretty flowers! Smell the pretty flowers!" they would urge. He stared, contrarily, at these disturbingly ominous vagaries, at these indistinct revelations from out of the dark mournful ground.

Years later, when as an adult bent on remembrance, he first addressed the nature of such childhood experiences, he inclined, at once, to invoke a theory of instinctual knowledge for his suspicions. He considered his uncanny precocious awareness of unseen but impending and fatally threatening circumstance, to be another of the seemingly automatic ways or divining talents of the species some how to have found its way into the genes and gotten to be passed along, generation after generation, as a behavioral entry bonus, a sort of evolutionary head start. Its under standing made it possible to know human conduct and behavioral patterns in part as nondescript echoes of all of that ancient suffering and successful innovation. All the same, because what is not entirely understood can be fear some as well as awesome, it was tempting to dispel his disturbing insights with any kind of reason, however hastily contrived. And so, important disclosures he had stumbled over, or rather, in his case unearthed, were all too easily buried again under the weight of a possibly imperfect logic, shaped quickly out of urgent need. Any thing now to stay composed. But he never did achieve through reason the measure of ease required. All he accomplished with his fancy theories was to rebury certain awful premonitions and yet have them still to haunt him.

Digging at things, always digging. It would become his steady state of mind. That obsession started up in the garden of his father's aunt. And wondering. Wondering why nothing was right. Wondering why, for example, from the outset he felt so old. Too old certainly to be as small as he was and to be put to sleep at night in a crib. Too small for the way he thought. And too small also, for at least a brief while, to be courted by his mother. Courted with toys, and special trips to movie theaters and restaurants, and ardently offered help with lessons, until he was in love. Love, however it matures, always starts out sexual. And this kind, a boy's love for his mother, soon becomes afflicted by apprehension for its ending. Such a good feeling it had been, and then almost immediately, his hopes and unclear expectations were dashed. He was old enough to sense trouble and yet too young to know what it was about. There was nowhere to turn for answers, but he was beginning on his own to grasp that there was something that gave, and almost as soon as it did so, everything was snatched away. In this early perception of the order of things, there was more than a hint of what would follow.

Now reconciled to sleeping again, even though he risked another harsh arousal, he chanced to think of his dead parents. No solace there. No comfort in the memory of their love or their sacrifices undergone doggedly in his behalf. He recalled their gestures, voices, smiles, laughs, remonstrances, cautionings, and shared times of every kind and variety. No pleasure for him in any of it. To the contrary, just sadness, grief, foreboding.

And before he fell asleep that second time, more of the agony which had to be there for a reason, took him over. After all, did not everything have to have a reason? So pain which must have purpose was imposed by the terrible reminder that those two people, his mother and his father, were forever lost to him. They were absolutely, unconditionally withdrawn from his experience as they were from all of life. Even the fragments of them he might glimpse in the faces of close relatives, or the reflections and the sounds of them he sensed in himself, were no more than the cruelly designed, fragmentary reincarnations of their derelict, reminding, pleading parts. To see, to know, to feel, to wonder, his parents would never do any of that again, or be anything for him or to each other. Soon, with his own passing, they would not even be a memory. For he had no children of his own.

Nor were his feelings improved by cemetery visits.

Grave-side tricks of recollection might be kindly mustered to make such spectacles rewarding for others. They were not so for him. When he stared at headstones, in the hope of seeing beyond them and back to better times, there was only the hideous image of rotting corpses, grotesquely deformed, offensive vestiges of what had once been a delight to behold. To call people dead was only shallow attempt to blur the awful reality. Dead people, including his parents, were not dead or anything else. They simply were not, any more.

Two

It was hard to understand, after nights like that, how the days which followed could be entered into so matter-of-factly. As if the morning light was born of its own optimism and gladdened everything it fell upon, including the ways in which even this man considered things. In truth, he had reached the point of banking on the morning brightness to bail him out of his customary nocturnal dol drums and anxieties. Perhaps that consoling power of the light derived from times when light was first life giving. Whatever was responsible for this abomination of existence did not pull it off out of nothing, covertly, under cover of darkness, he would muse. It was started up surely, in the glare of day. So ripples of light heartedness might be tracked all the way back through time to the consequence of that fiendishly intended first luminosity and be swept into the present as the deceptively blinding cheer of mere being. For certain, a blissful blinding to the basic darkness of reality was a necessary condition if the business of life was to be kept going.

It was thus he speculated while shaving the next morning. That is not to say that a relative sense of early hour buoyancy precluded his having other thoughts most would take to be quite morbid. For example, what would be the kindest time for this fearing and resentful man to die? Better surely to die at night, when everything to be given up was hidden in the shadows, not blazing away to an illusory hopeful infinity, ever the false lure. Better to die in the gloom of night, when one was already half back to primal darkness, that time when the Action was not yet taken, and perhaps not even conceived.

He dressed and took breakfast in the usual manner. Spousal leave-taking was necessarily brief as his wife had taken to staying in bed nowadays until late morning. This had been going on for almost a year. Finally, he began the drive down Connecticut Avenue. Back to the hospital for him, back to tinkering in the electroencephalography lab. Back to brain waves, computers, oscilloscopes, and endless sheets and rolls of graph paper to which the normal, the demented, the epileptic, the half paralyzed, imparted the slightly variable imprint of electrical activity discharged from their brain surfaces. When he had first started out in his medical career, even earlier while still taking his degrees, he'd had the foolish idea there would be important things to be read someday from out of all of those ink-penned squiggles made by human brains on slowly crawling paper. There might even be a way to fathom thought processes.

Nothing of the sort! Sometimes at very best, he might confirm the presence of epilepsy, or find that something debilitating, but never specific, was going on in one side of the brain, or that a patient was only comatose but not electrocortically silenced, what was known as being brain dead. If he should manage to get lucky with his own experimental use of computers, the only reward would be a machine that made these probably unimportant clinical distinctions that a well-trained technician with a high school education or less, could make by merely glancing at the slowly moving paper. So after all his years of advanced learning, to be Adam Turner the electroencephalographer, was to his mind perfectly consistent with a sense of winding up as not much of anything at all.

But when he had begun at this, it was still all very exciting. It was a foray into the unknown, and it helped to distract him from his inclination to ruminate on unpleasant matters, like the one of time running out. It gave meaning to his life, a sense of purpose, and it was easy to transpose such an attitude to the idea that life itself had some kind of meaning. But now the work had become a bore. Oh, sure, there were other people out there doing the same sort of thing, who were just thrilled to be riveted to their computers. To his mind, however, they surely needed precious little to sustain their pleasurable sense of significance if all of their endless, pedestrian, recording and note taking could engender so much fascination for them. Be sides, he now had his own idea about the so called meaningful, and how to take his pleasure.

Not long after he had begun to formulate his thoughts on that score, he had come upon a statement by Albert Einstein which he took to be remarkable and which also piqued him considerably. The great man had opined that anyone believing life to be meaningless was not only unfortunate, but also "almost disqualified for life." What cheek! Such hubris! No wonder, he reflected at the time, that what had obviously become a limited and narrow mind never did manage to come up with its long-sought after unitary theory of the universe!

To his own thinking, the thinking of this electro-encephalographer, the problem was precisely that man, like every other creature, had been eminently and craftily designed for life alone but not at all for its denial, its negation, for nothingness and death. And death itself was made too shocking, too awful, for penetration to its essence or its origin. Therefore, quite automatically, it came to be repressed, denied, or trivialized by behavioral reflex, general agreement, even legislative provision; or made a mystery through religion. All this, not only to assure a tidy, endurable kind of life, but also so that the end of life might account for life's pain, give it its "meaning." That seemed to be the Plan. But oddly, besides the readiness to flee death, to affirm life, and to assign almost any kind of meaning to life, by some peculiar fluke or oversight man had been gifted with what Einstein could only see as a fatal failing, but which was really a salvation of sorts: By the most tortuous mental straining, man could still some how manage to renounce life and by its rejection experience an intensity of living that gave the devil his due. To spurn life, to declare it meaningless, to refuse to participate in its compulsive and unending routine, was only to have it fight back and try to overwhelm with the enormity of its allurements. The Thing could be tricked. But concede to life just what was arranged for in the Plan and what you got were too many stars, so many monotonous grains of sand, always another challenge to understanding. Riddles within and beyond riddles. Einstein's quest was really no more than his ensnarement, a life sentence to workaday, dutiful mole-digging, fancifully passed off by him as an exhilarating engagement of the unknown. Farfetched, ignorantly conceitful! His antics were remindful of nothing so much as the poor chase dog hell bent after the artificial lure deceptively and cruelly attached to its very own nose. What real mystery, anyway, could there be in a succession of endless questions doomed to be pursued each in its turn forever? Better the ending of that search in some merciful blind alley, but mercy was not the name of this game!

Now who might think, to see this conventionally dressed and well-behaved fellow in his middle years so conscientiously at work, seemingly engrossed in reporting the electroencephalographic tracings of the previous day, or peering into empty space, the better presumably to be undistracted while dictating his reports, that he was scarcely mindful at all of what he was doing. His actions, in fact, were rote. His mind might be away on silly Einstein, for example, or how he planned to spend his midday break, conveniently passed off as time for lunch. Work may completely capture the body, but not the mind, and there's as much all-consuming self interest going on behind the pointedly focussed stare as behind a vacant look. So at the end of this particular morning the electroencephalographer exchanged his white lab coat for a tweed jacket and departed the hospital seeking a sort of treatment for his mood, well thought out in advance, and of a somewhat better kind than could be afforded by mere chance exposure to the upbeat light of day.

He was off again to Connecticut Avenue, but this time by cab and not north to Chevy Chase, which was home. He was headed south, away from the woman in the next bed who slept very well each night, and much of the morning also, after too much drink. He could not find the required treatment there. It was to be dispensed in the apartment of a different woman, who was a bit younger, and who could not drink at night because that was when she worked, as a nurse. This arrangement, in place about a month, was both casual and theoretical. Casually was the way he had found the young woman who did not drink. He had met her at a Christmas party. Theoretically and deliberately was the way he was using her.

The theory was simple enough to understand. If a person inclined to bouts of depression finds out it isn't possible to be both depressed and sexually active at the same moment, the solution, at least a temporary one, fairly begs of discovery. That is so if one does not fancy being constantly depressed. And if the woman sharing his bed, because of alcohol abuse, no longer cares much for sex, her downcast husband may decide to seek elsewhere for his special remedy.

That is why, when he turned the key at Connecticut South, the electroencephalographer's mind was not set on romance or other open-ended diversion. He was remembering, rather, that there exist certain provocative pleasure centers in the hypothalamus of the brain which, once fired up, operate to the exclusion of all other feelings, particularly those inclined to get a person down. For sure, no ordinary lovelorn fellow would be entering a woman's apartment with little more on his mind than the euphoria of certain experimental rats, who privileged by clever surgical positioning of wires in those same pleasure centers of the brain, could be titillated around the clock, oblivious to all other appetites and desires, including even those basic ones for sleep and for food. Of course, he never dared confess such mental meanderings to the young woman who did not drink or he'd soon be having to look else where for what he required.

On making entry there was the sound of water pounding in a tub. The bathroom door was ajar. He called through the half cracked doorway.

"You in there?"

"Did you expect someone else? Be out in a while."

Dammit! Not what he expected.

"Why don't I just join you?"

No point to sitting alone in the next room and wasting valuable time. His idea was to salvage the better part of thirty minutes she would probably be inaccessible to him, and so rather quickly he was in the tub beside her and sort of being welcomed.

"Well, well, look whom I've run into!"

"My pleasure."

He wasn't joking. It was comforting to recline there while she pummelled them both with hot water from the tap. Even better, she brought special talents to bear, as good little nurse that she was, she began to wash and to massage him, stroking, pulling, and kneading, in a way that left his limbs drained and his mind, for once, briefly thoughtless. The dragged-out gnawing pleasure was in tense, hypnotic. Nothing else mattered. He could stay like that, contemplating the merit of either lunging for a gratifying release, or hanging suspended, close on to it. It could be however he chose. It wasn't his intention to demean her. Only that his actions and thoughts were ruled by his special need.

Abruptly, however, in her workaday efficient manner, she declared tub time over, pulled the stopper, vaulted erect, and disappeared into a wrap of toweling. The water rushing out, his flesh no longer warmed and floated, skin folds hanging unsupported, uncomforted, he felt a sense of exaggerated weight upon him, bearing, forcing, him down. To where? Also, there was an unkindly cold intrusive draft. It wasn't good to be laid out like this in the raw, in the suddenly unfriendly confines of an empty tub, now more like some kind of porcelain tank. Did he remember such a tank? Could it be for embalming? Who reclined beside it? Or in it? It was Marty Ackerman, his classmate, dead at thirteen from appendicitis! And the electroencephalographer was back with all those other students being dragged along by Mrs. MacQuaid, their elderly teacher, over to Marty's house just as he was being laid out. He still couldn't remember whether good old Marty lay along side or was actually in the tank when he bade him that last farewell. He did recall, though, how ashen cold his friend had looked. Now the electroencephalographer jumped up, even more quickly than had the young nurse, dried off, and bolted for the next room to join her in bed.

"It's just sex, isn't it, Adam?" Her question after that quite unavoidable event.

"Why trivialize what was terrific?"

"You're using me."

"Well, I couldn't have managed it without you!"

"That's just what I mean, you bastard! You have no idea at all of what it is to really be with someone, do you?"

"I thought we did pretty well. And unless I'm mistaken, we were really together when we were pulling it off!"

"That's not how it's supposed to be. I don't just hopping into bed with anyone. It's supposed to be about some thing."

"Well neither do I. One can't be too careful these days. But thanks for the compliment."

There was hardly any point, thought the electroencephalographer, to start up on the bare-bones meaning of human sexuality. It had been his own inclination to put it in the category of physical needs, and nowadays, his access to mood elevation. Not that he didn't like Maureen. She was damned good looking, and if only she wouldn't, like just about everyone else, get off on this everlasting business of having to justify, moralize, or make somehow significant, every simple little yen, they could be having a reasonably good time of it together. It had been, after all, what he took for a vivaciousness, as well as her physical essentials, that had attracted him to her in the first place. As it was, she was hell bent now upon spoiling every thing. But hell bent without being devil may care!

He had played light and been therefore irreverent about sex, to her something oddly sacred.

"May God forgive you!"

Damn it! Now he was going to pay dearly for his sex therapy thing. The whole business was about to unravel. Even there, next to her, under the heavy covers, he began to feel cold again, estranged. This cute little bird, staring pensively at something on the ceiling, as if it were celestial and much beyond them, was setting to go religious. He tried to draw her back.

"Please pray to yourself. Don't let me in on it. I'll respect you and I won't bother you. Do we have a deal?"

"I really think that if only you could believe, accept God, you could be a happy person. And not be so self centered, so, so ... creepy!"

"Please, Maureen, don't take away the only things I've got. All I have is me, the way I am, and a total incapacity as far as any kind of religious leaning goes."

She wasn't hearing him. Not one bit. It was time again for her to save his soul. The return of melancholia was beginning to seem a pleasant alternative to what, undoubtedly, was coming next. Anything to divert her.

"Think you'll get that pay raise?"

"You're not listening to me, Adam."

"Anything more about the morphine business?"

Seems that in her hospital five vials of morphine were missing from the ward medicine cabinet, to which on night shifts, only she had the keys. The bird had an idea some one "may" have "borrowed" them. Anyway, she was in hot water. Could even wind up getting fired and lose her license. But she was on one of her fervent rolls, brushing even that impending catastrophe aside.

"If you would just know Him and stop trying to figure every little thing out. It's not possible to know His mind."

"You think He might know how the morphine disappeared?"

"Don't get smart. If only you could understand. Of course He knows. He knows everything. He sees every thing."

No use. She was beyond either distraction or recall, but he was not about to cave.

"Well then, you can save yourself a heap of trouble.

Just ring Him up. Maybe He'll even testify in your behalf as a character witness if they bring you up on charges!"

She was not to be deterred. "That's not the way it works."

"It works?"

"Of course it does, silly! I know I'm going to be all right. Just believing is enough. Believing in Him and His word and His ways. His infinite goodness. He's there to save us all, no matter what. Try it. You might just find yourself feeling better."

"What about those three drive-by shootings last night? Two people got themselves killed. Think He heard about that or the four-year-old who shot her father in the head? And does He know that between Iran, Iraq, and Ethiopia they say at least a thousand starving kids are setting to take off from planet earth every day this year? That's be sides the two percent of earth's people now down with aids."

"It is not for us to know the mystery of His ways. There's a good reason for everything. We are not to know them or to judge Him."

"Well if He's really out there somewhere, I say it's high time we did. He's getting away with some big time murder. I was just thinking yesterday when I was in the john, what is there, really, to stop someone from coming up behind me and shooting me square in the back of my head, right in the middle of a leak? Not Him surely!"

"You're terrible!"

Then nothing more from her. She drew herself up on a pillow, reached for a cigarette, and blew her first puff toward the heavenly above, which she scrutinized as if seeking some kind of sign. It was his cue and as good a time as any to take his leave. Tobacco made him sick. Besides, she had to get to sleep soon anyway. Her shift began at eleven and it was already two thirty. He showered and dressed. She remained in bed.

"Take care, Maureen."

"You think about what I said!"

"Right, you might just have something there."

He lied, but it was in a good cause. The now troubled young nurse with the gift of faith smiled and lit up finally to hear him say it. Marvelous, that gift! Somehow there was supposed to be a special beneficence in how it was dispensed among those growing up in families that packed the young ones, fresh out the cradle, through all those suckering church doors. As for the smile; on a face like hers, who could ask for more? Problem was, from out all that cuteness also came all of this absolute drivel. It was enough to have him back down again as he headed away. No point in finishing out his day in the laboratory. He didn't have to, so he wouldn't. Or at least he didn't think he had to. And even if he had known that one of the psychiatry residents was in fact inquiring after him, he'd hardly have gone back just for something like that. It was the one beauty of what he held to be his inconsequential work. There were no electroencephalographic emergencies. He strolled for an hour, then decided on the National Portrait Gallery.

Three

It was a favorite place. Here he could get down to serious thinking and maybe consult a bit. Also, there were very few visitors to disturb him on weekdays. It was his habit to walk about awhile, returning stares with this or that framed personage, and then settle on whomever might seem most compatible with what his state of mind happened to be at the moment. Then, he'd silently air his notions of the day, never bothering to read the captions and to find out who his particular painted confidante was supposed to be. He generally preferred anonymity. It was just better not to know one another. Anyway, the electroencephalographer wouldn't want to find out he'd emptied his heart and mind to some sort of fellow in capable of understanding him, an 1829-or-other low life.

But that afternoon, considering what he'd just been put through by the bird, he chose to search the gallery walls for a minister of sorts, or anyone with what might be taken for a clerical collar. He sat down before a seemingly good old fellow, thinking that the man wore a kind enough face and liked especially the way his eyes returned his own stare in an honest, straightforward manner. Yes, quite good, the eyes were properly converged and aimed directly on him. Not inattentive, far away, lackadaisical, or cockeyed like the looks peculiar to portraits by almost all of the naive artists.

"All right, let's have at it," was his opening thought. "Things have not been going well. Not last night. Not today either. I feel I'm under a really urgent need to re group, to reorganize my thinking, to formulate some kind of game plan for going on that is philosophically consistent with whatever reasonable conclusions I've been able to draw after all these years of sifting through everything ad nauseam. OK?"

Seemed quite sensible to the old boy up there. No sign of demurral.

"For our purpose, here today, I'm willing to forget entirely the issues of meaninglessness and the question of why anything at all. Why not, for example, as has been asked, just nothing? This existence thing just hits on me entirely too hard--not often, but once and a while too hard, to write it off as an utter fluke, or a miracle without meaning, or a miracle without even a miracle maker. That word, by the way, should be used sparingly. If it's used too much, absolutely mind boggling happenings can get to seem quite ordinary. For example, look at what's going on over there in Ireland! They've got tears popping out of every little village statue of the Virgin! We just can't be having round the clock, round the corner miracles, can we?" The old one seemed to stir just a bit. Was he possibly a papist type? Best not take any chances.

"Now, I'm not being at all inconsistent, mind you, with what I was thinking back in the lab only today about silly Einstein. My difficulty with him is that he wrote me off completely. If you remember, he said I wasn't qualified to live. And how come that's supposed to be so? Well, because I just don't happen to look at things in the same upbeat or even neutral way that he does. Einstein really set me off with that one! So Father, if you'll excuse the expression, God damn him, but life is too much of a downer for me to buy his view of things. I'm determined, nevertheless, to live on anyway. I make no bones about my resolution to do that whether or not Mr. Einstein happens to consider me eligible for survival. That's the deal even if I should almost die every night much as I did last night. Even if I get absolutely no jollies from this living thing. I'm in it for keeps, for whatever my duration. So don't you worry about some fool move on my part, like me committing suicide. OK?"

The church, of course, had no taste for such inclinations. So far, so good.

"To come, finally, to the point, Father, if I may continue to call you that. I seem always to have had the most peculiar feeling that I know things I'm really not at all supposed to know. I've come up with a few fancy theories on it; but if the truth were to be known, and it's always high time for that, I don't have any real enthusiasm for any of them. I can't imagine why I know these things, and beyond that, I don't even know what it is that I seem to know. Top that one if you will! I just haven't a clue, really, to what's going on. Downright baffling! And the funniest thing, well not really funny at all, but when I have these thoughts, or sensations, or whatever the hell, excuse me, this stuff is, just like when I was a kid, I seem to hear music."

The framed one was looking somewhat uncomfortable. Like maybe some kind of a nut had him cornered up on that wall.

"Now, I don't really even mean music. It's just that when I have this thing going on, this peculiar knowing thing, every sound and voice I hear is kind of remote, oddly intoned, inflected, distorted, irrelevant. When I was a kid I would simply say everybody sounded funny. Know what I mean? But lately I've been thinking this could be some kind of disturbance in my brain. Like in some of my epileptic patients with problems in their temporal lobes. Some choice, huh? I'm either possessed or brain damaged!

"Well, now here's the problem. I just can't for the life of me (and that's what it's all about, the life of me and this music when I think about what the life of me amounts to) imagine how you (and being a minister or what not, I take you to be fairly representative of what is called the faith) can expect to be considered seriously, if you'll excuse an other expression, about what I call the party line."

This audience could quite quickly come to an end. "As I understand it, the story goes that we are supposed to be settled into what is called the vale of tears. Not a very opportune place by the way, for someone like me, a fellow who has never in his entire life been able to cry. Anyway, because of good works it doesn't have to be all crying time here anymore. We can turn this place into a veritable heaven on earth. We really don't need to aspire to anything better. We can ride things out right here and be damned, excuse me, happy for it. We do it by living according to the good book and by praying. But if some how things just don't happen to work out that agreeably, then by those same good works, earth is guaranteed any way to become a sort of opportune jumping off place, like a launch site for that, shall we say, eternal soft landing. But Father, something's wrong. I smell a rat. Like, besides us, who needs all this and why? For us it's either-or, if you get what I mean. And it's all going to happen not because we actually want to live that way, but because it must be so and in His name, or else! In short, if I'm to go along with it, seems to me I should know why He needs all this.

After all, He's putting us through a helluva lot (excuse me, I intend no irreverence) to have His way."

Now, the electroencephalographer did not really expect a response from the framed fellow up on the wall. This was just his way of going through the motions of a discussion he'd be much too embarrassed to have with a real live person. It was something, though, that he was very much impelled to do. It could shape and sharpen his thinking. Even point him in new directions.

"So, sir, just what kind of superforce are we dealing with and how come it's got these oddball needs? Like I say, we are expected to act in ways that are not entirely natural to us. We were not made with such sure-fire, goody-goody inclinations, or at least not disposed to having them override those that are more self-serving, but for His plea sure, or purpose, or whatever, we're supposed to exercise the will, to just go ahead and do it, get His job done. And for Him that's the signal that morally and worshipfully we've arrived. Joined what might be called the ecclesiastical in-crowd.

"Seems to me this fellow, I mean God, could have straight forwardly set about creating us to do things right in the first place, and we'd all of us gotten along just fine. But no, we're saddled with a God who has either plain and simple screwed up or who has to be indulged to the point of, excuse me just one more liberty, idolatry, or as you might say, adoration. But for what? His power? His perfection? If that were really so, he wouldn't need all of this!

"And look at all the pain and suffering brought on us poor Christians while trying to pull this thing off. Not to mention the agonies and perplexities reserved for all those poor slobs in other cultures and religions, the outsiders with not even a blessed clue as to what's going on.

"Which raises a couple of other possibilities. After all, that's what we're trying to examine, the possibilities, right?"

Dead, maybe even deadly silence.

"So let's suppose we've got it all wrong. Suppose that instead of being Mr. Nice Guy this is a god who evolved us for no other reason but that he enjoys watching us suffer. Now we've really got a problem. No way out of that one. No salvation, certainly. The whole thing nothing but a sick trick. Just a bad rap for all of us, the would-be insiders and the outsiders, both."

It seemed that perhaps his grim direction and cynicism were being seriously considered by the other one.

"Or maybe His power is kind of limited and this whole thing has got to be worked out in stages, like one of our own creations. And we're just an intermediate phase. You know, like a kind of test model."

The electroencephalographer paused and then continued.

"Father, none of this quite makes sense, does it? There's just got to be a better kind of miracle if that's what we're really into. That is, if all of this is actually about anything at all. I've got my own humble opinion on it, and I've been stewing over this for a long, long time."

The old fellow with collar, frame and all, seemed maybe to be leaning a bit further into the room below, as if not wanting to miss out on what the electroencephalographer had hit upon.

"Now, I want you to know I don't have it quite entirely straight. It's all mixed up with the music thing. Odd how when I hear my voice kind of thinking through all of this, it can get so muddled up with all of the sing-songing and the high tones and whatnot going on simultaneously, I can't make out my very own thoughts too well. But I've got at least the vague outline of it. I know I'm onto something."

The painting remained tilted forward, now more expectantly?

"But it would be much too premature to present even the broad sweep of my theory to you right now, Father. And it wouldn't be at all proper to air wild guesses either. I'm trained, you know, as a scientist. We don't simply speculate. There's the need, above all, to be scrupulously rigid with one's methods if one is to be on solid ground, or anywhere else, right? You know very well that even in your own field, Father, like before you ministers finally get to say that something's really written, so to speak, there's often been an awful lot of good solid observation and reporting by all kinds of folk. Well, that's the way it is for us scientific fellows too, but every time and all the time, Father. We don't say anything until we're, forgive me, Goddarnned sure of it. But I just know it's coming! And I have a fair idea of what it is. I'll give you a little hint. We may not be quite where we think we are!"

By then it was late afternoon. The rumble of early evening rush hour traffic could be heard mounting in the street outside. It could actually be felt within the building. That was probably why the heavily framed painting vibrated and seemed to tremble as the electroencephalographer left the gallery.

Four

His intention had been to cab back to the hospital, pick up his car, and head home. Instead, he found himself walking. Christmas was but two weeks away. The shops were brightly decorated and beginning to fill with foraging buyers. The circumstances were just right for making observations of people as they made their way about town through the narrow corridors of space and time allowed them.

First off, no one looked the least bit cheerful, and secondly, there was a tremendous variety of just about everything in the store windows. As for the pervasive solemnity, so ill befitting this particular season, it was not an aberration to be expected and borne of currently hard economic times. It had always been like that. He had made a study of it and knew it to be so. People always looked about the same, whether it was time, as now, to celebrate the birth of a savior or to mourn his death, whether or not he was resurrected. Something forever weighed upon them. And any person grinning from ear to ear, or cheerfully yakking it up, seemed an out of place oddball. That kind of man or woman would startle the others. Theirs would be a poorly concealed amazement followed by a turning away. They could not bear that kind of lunacy.

These were things he knew not only from his own personal observations over many years, but also from archival photographs of crowds and vintage newsreel footages going back as long as such technology existed. Faces in a crowd, by every reasonable expectation should show the variety of human expressions; instead they looked consistently crestfallen. Mass celebrations of the new year or of victory in war, as well as public scenes of sporting events or mourning, were of course excluded from his data base, but they were the only exceptions. No doubt about it. Exuberance had never been much around.

So here were all these very glum people looking at all these things that could be bought. There was a consistency of excesses; the moroseness of the people and the number of things for sale. But it would be hard to figure out any truly significant differences among the items. Aesthetics aside, if one just looked at utilitarian things, like television sets or CD players, what real advantages could be discerned among them? Obviously, they weren't worth being bothered over. The CD players would all sound the same. The TV screen images were pretty much alike. Most of the gross national product, however, depended upon people worrying over how to make their choices from out of all that sameness. The manufacturers and the advertising people, to the electroencephalographer's thinking, probably knew more about what drove people into those bursting stores than the psychiatrists. They were in business by grace of trading on that very knowledge. All these poor miserable shoppers were after was meaning, any meaning they could arrange for. If they could only buy something new, anything, no matter how dumb it was, to take home and glory in for a while, they'd manage to make them selves different, from what they were before and also possibly different from the guy next door. They needed that. It made life meaningful. It was a pretty sad state of affairs. They had to find new toys in order to have a sense of worth for their lives. And the meaning? It was that owning something new was to be new. It was to be born again. Manage to keep that up, and you never die! How monstrous, this futile attempt to evade the inevitable!

Staring into a shop window featuring fifty kinds of running shoe the electroencephalographer could not but marvel over what philosophers and psychiatrists did man age to have in common with the purveyors of that abundance. People were being urged by all of them to go out and get meaning in their lives by doing or buying some thing new. That's what was needed to counter feelings of depression in a world sensed finally as devoid of any meaning of its own. And they'd best be about it post haste if they were to have any decent moments before their time was up. Moreover, this was something to be done without witness, because God, if ever he did exist, and there was absolutely no evidence for that, was now quite dead. So better buy yet one more trinket or holiday in still some other place, before it was all too late.

This, in a nutshell, was the theory and the philosophy of existentialism. Not something which had ever had much appeal for the electroencephalographer. What that bit of hokum assumed was that people could deliberately con themselves. Every time he heard the existential approach urged upon someone, he'd think about how certain cows were accounted to jump over just about any old moon. Cows and people did not work the impossible. Nor did they perform miracles. People might be good at tricking one another. They generally weren't much for knowingly fooling themselves. Good perhaps for using distractions to ward off reality, sure, but for making meaning where there was none? A ridiculous expectation!

Philosophy had always been a problem for him. It seemed not to have much coin for those who revelled in it, if everyone else could understand it. He often doubted whether the philosopher himself understood precisely what he was saying. On the other hand, what the electroencephalographer said was usually very, very clear to him. Maybe that would not make it good philosophy, but it was something for him to keep building upon. If, in fact, he ever did get quite to the point of not understanding exactly what he was saying, then at the risk of being that "philosophical," he'd have to strike out in some other direction. Of course there were certain times when what he said did happen to have little to do with what he was actually thinking. But that was only when his thoughts were being muddled by the music thing, which as yet was not at all comprehensible. He'd have to wait before passing final judgment on that.

As he studied the swelling numbers of passersby he took note of the ways in which they seemed to accommodate one another. Either they ignored all those around them so pointedly one could be certain they were actually taking everything in, or they stole furtive looks at each other, managing to stare and yet avoid meeting anyone else's countering gaze. He could not even begin to fathom how this was accomplished; it would seem to call for some uncanny extra sense. And the other thing was that the ones who worked this surreptitious eyeing back and forth apparently had no taste for what they saw.

He had wondered at one time if the reasons for this distaste could be racial. The electroencephalographer was long convinced that racially founded aversions are quite fixed biologically and never really overcome. They were sort of evolutionary hand-me-downs, locked in way back when it was very much in the self interest to be wary of whomever looked different. But no, that wasn't it at all.

This prevalent register of ill regard was only a tad less directed toward someone of one's own kind as toward an "other." He was dead sure of this. He even had statistics to prove it. They were established irrefutably one sunny afternoon when he was sitting by himself on a bench in Dupont Circle. With a little counter in the left hand, he clicked off how blacks and whites viewed each other and then by a right handed counter-how blacks or whites regarded themselves. The results were unassailable. No body seemed to like or to trust anyone else irrespective of what kind of person the other happened to be.

Things were not any different in the place he now stood, even though it would soon be Christmas, than they had been months before in a Dupont Circle fairly brimming over with antipathy. What could possibly be the relevance of the electroencephalographer's seemingly eccentric acumen? Quite a lot. Putting it all together, it meant to him that given the general state of human guardedness and hostility, any person he might incline to like, might turn to, and who could find it in themselves to reciprocate his reaching out, was indeed a rare find, a veritable treasure. All things considered, such a person might finally prove to be his only treasure. And this particular season made for no variance. The world at large, certainly the one down town, yuletide or no yuletide, was an uneasy place to be. It was time to return home to his wife.

The electroencephalographer looked for a taxi. He needed a ride back to the hospital to pick up his car still parked there since morning.

But a strange person stood in his way.

"Hey, mister! You know President Roosevelt and the secret service are lookin' for you?"

The man was dressed as a soldier but could never pass for the real thing. He did wear green fatigues, field boots and a combat helmet. But from the top of the helmet trailed at least a fifteen foot length of red silk ribbon secured at its end to an old pair of rusty scissors which dragged along behind him on the sidewalk. Shorter lengths of blue and yellow ribbon were tied around his arms at the elbow. He was a happy sort, grinning with satisfaction, it seemed, to share this confidence of his with the electroencephalographer who had decided to hear him out.

"Why would Roosevelt and the secret service want to come looking for me?"

"You drive a Cadillac! They're on to everyone in a Cadillac!"

Then he laughed. Laughed so hard his eyes began to water.

"But I don't drive a Cadillac. I drive a Ford. In fact, my car isn't even here. It's 'crosstown where I left it."

"You don't know anything. They always leave you empty handed and they never hang around. That's for sure." Then, more laughter. An infectious kind of laughter which the electroencephalographer considered very appealing. Why here was a fellow with completely scrambled brain connections who was having himself such a wonderful time! Neither what went on around him nor what came off in his own completely mixed up head could manage to get this fellow down! What a lucky guy!

"I like your uniform. Were you in Vietnam?"

"How long did it take you?"

"To do what?"

"You shouldn't shoot yourself."

"I look dead? Is that what you think?"

"Roosevelt doesn't care if they shoot you."

Then the schizophrenic soldier stepped in front of a young woman at the curb. She had been waiting her chance to cross the busy street but now found herself trapped suddenly by this quite insane man. He, still smiling, pointed to the electroencephalographer and demanded an answer from her.

"Shall we hire him, sister? If we don't, they'll sure as hell send him over! Over there!"

The woman seized on her first opportunity to take off as the soldier came closer. She could have been run down, starting to cross as she did, before the light changed, in order to stay clear of him. Could it be the case, thought the electroencephalographer, that what really frightened her was the man's smiling manner? Around here, it was so out of place, wasn't it?

The woman gone, the grinning one turned once more toward the electroencephalographer.

"It could happen!"

"What's that?"

"You should know. Don't you always know? It's time for a haircut. That's what! Shall I go to sleep and have one?"

"It's too cold out here for anyone to be taking a nap. Besides I have to go for my car right now or I'll be late for dinner. Remember? The Ford, back in the parking lot near the hospital."

"I had breakfast once."

"Take care sergeant!"

"I have a guitar you know!"

"Play a tune for me!"

That suggestion had the man laughing again, laughing once more to the point of tears. As the electroencephalographer hailed down a cab, the soldier, ribbons trailing behind him, stepped out into the middle of the street and drew a half full bottle of orange soda from a jacket pocket. Traffic had come to a halt and the crazy guy was holding his orange pop aloft as if to toast a driver who had been forced to stop his car no more than a foot short of him.

"Hey! Hey you! C'mon let's party! But first let's go to the pentagon and pick up Roosevelt! OK, old buddy?"

The electroencephalographer pulled away in his cab, watched through the window as the joyous soldier, ribbons swirling around him, continued to block traffic. Nice to know a person could feel so irrelevantly swell! But how might you pull off something like that if you weren't as bizarre as he? What was there to be appropriately happy about in his own peculiar world?

In a few minutes he was in the hospital parking lot. He found his car where he had left it in the morning. As he slid behind the wheel he was called out to from behind. "Adam!"

It was the dean of the college of medicine. The electroencephalographer worked in a hospital affiliated with a medical school.

"Hi Doctor Carson."

"I've been meaning to drop you a memorandum, Adam. Any problem if I put you on the institutional re view board?"

The institutional review board or I.R.B., as it was called, served a watchdog function for clinical research involving human subjects. It was supposed to assure that patients were properly informed as to the dangers facing them when they consented to experimental treatments, but also that they were not induced in any way to volunteer and had full knowledge of alternative, more conventional ways they might also be treated should they not want to be experimented upon.

"Why me? Somebody quit or die?"

"No. It's just that things are getting bogged down. The way I see it, there's just too much nit-picking going on. We need someone in there who knows how to keep things moving along. Someone like you who's real efficient. These other men don't seem to get it that every research proposal we can expedite and that winds up being funded, brings in money the school can really use right now."

If the electroencephalographer happened to seem "efficient," it was only because he didn't want to spend any more time than was absolutely necessary at work he no longer considered important. Besides, he needed time for his outside activities, from some of which he was at this very moment returning.

"I'm not your man, Doctor Carson."

"Why not?"

"Because I've always considered that whole review set up a phony business. No matter what they claim in those research proposals, they're gonna do what they want to do, anyway. To get patients to volunteer, doctors promise them the bloody moon, and as for risks or alternatives, even if they knew exactly what they were, which they don't, they wouldn't let anybody in on them! Informed patient consent is a joke around here! Like I say, it's a phony business through and through."

"Come on, Adam, that's ridiculous! Look, you take this job and you're excused from all your other committee and faculty meetings. That ought to make you happy! And I'll be happy too! You want us both to be happy, don't you? Be a good boy and please your old dean! What do you say? Have we got a deal? You move those I.R.B. guys along just like you hustle that EEG department of yours and everything will work out fine! How about it?"

"I can be happy doing something I think is crazy?"

"Why sure, son! We both can!"

"Well, to tell the truth, I just met someone who thinks likes you do. But he's more endowed than we are."

"Who would that be?"

"He's in the military. Well, okay, Doctor Carson, suit yourself. But don't forget to put that other stuff in writing. You know, what you said about me not having to bother with any other faculty meetings or committee work from here on in."

"No sooner said than done, Adam! Thank you! Tonight, you have me going home a relaxed and happy man!" Funny thing! Every time the electroencephalographer thought about going crazy, it worried him. It worried him a lot. Maybe he had been wrong to feel that way. Because here were these two happy men, seemingly onto some thing neat. And no doubt about it, they were sure as hell, the soldier and this dean, both of them, absolutely nuts!

Five

During twenty years of marriage, there was not a time that the electroencephalographer did not look forward to arriving home and seeing his wife. Were he to lose her, he doubted that he'd have any further inclination to pursue anything, particularly his work. He seemed to carry on only by the mere fact of her existence. As for the abstract way he directed most every thought, it was by dint of her indulging his fierce self-absorption. Only the secure and comfortable atmosphere she had until recently made possible permitted him the luxury of his convoluted ways. The measure of her love was more than amply demonstrated, not only by her incessant, embarrassing, voicing of it, but by her persistence as his devoted marital partner. She was always, and for the most part still remained, a woman of good cheer. But a few years back she'd had a shock. She discovered that she would not, as apparently she had taken for granted, live on forever. Of course when this was related to the electroencephalographer, a person not only thinking constantly about little else but death, its nature, meaning, and how somehow it might be put off, he wondered at first if she were spoofing him. But no, his wife was serious. Then he thought her mind was going, for which there was no precedent in either her prior behavior or the medical history of her immediate family. Before he could come up with some other reason, she gave him her own credible explanation. At least it had made sense to her and in time became plausible to him. His wife, the woman of almost unlimited joviality, had never thought about death in a self-directed way. The personal inevitability of death had not occurred to her because she'd had the surprising good fortune of not seeing it intervene in any of the lives around her. But quite unexpectedly, her sister, her twin, was killed in an auto accident. For a long while she was withdrawn and despondent. Then one gray overcast day, the kind he'd hardly expect to set the scene for resumption of her happy breezy ways, she was her old self again. He was forced to exclude either providence or spontaneous remission as explanations when he discovered that his wife, at least at night, was sipping wine to shore up her spirits. During those hours, which were sometimes the only ones they might have together, he would often retreat to some other room to avoid an argument over her drinking. It further weighed upon him (and he'd only learned of it after their marriage) that both her parents had been severe alcoholics.

There is no way for persons who do not drink on a

regular, daily basis to share in the jollity of those who do. Also, there's usually some resentment among sober bystanders toward what seems to be the inappropriate euphoria of drinkers. But in spite of his wife's addiction, the electroencephalographer continued to draw marital support and comfort during those hours when she did not drink. And after all, it was especially easy for someone like him to understand both her weakness and her motivations.

One way or another, as the electroencephalographer saw things, to suffer as little pain as possible, most people try to get themselves drunk on something. But not he. In the last few years he had assumed the obsessive resolve to forego anything that might cloud his perception of what he figured was the deadly nature of reality. He had to meet it head on and clear headed. If his wife took to drink it was not much different from what all the others were resorting to. To avoid their mortality, that life was no more than a death watch, they labored, played, drank, prayed. Every endeavor, every romance, every devious sublimation, every diversion, every musical harmony, every well turned phrase, every freshly invented dance step, each was needed to substitute for some other soon too commonplace, or too familiar distraction from the signs of life's slippage. All of this frenzied behavior, to his mind, was just so much casting about for ways to avoid confrontation with what was eventually going to happen. That was not to say he thought these antics were always deliberate; much of this creative excess and almost rabid pursuit of diversion derived from an instinct for self preservation. Fresh from infancy, this kind of flailing human conduct, instinctually-driven, becomes more and more manifest. Children, unlike adults, at first do not generally look wary and oppressed. But as soon as the fragile and brief nature of human existence begins to overwhelm them, they change. When the electroencephalographer first read that these ways of escaping reality were but sublimations of the sexual drive, or Dionysian celebrations of a life force, he was incredulous! How off the mark to take them for that. It was so obvious to him they were nothing more than a death dance, executed to evade the misery of the death watch!

But there could be no good haven for flesh sensing its own decline. People are warned of their end and yet by a mean design, denied an untroubled reverie of last delight. No way out there. No end stage gusto. The flesh is spared only the painful extremity of knowing precisely its final time and place. That ultimate cruelty is reserved for the ways of men towards men, and is not part of the deadly protocol of whatever it was to bring about time, that fiend ish creation for driving home a very painful lesson.

Home again.

"Hello love!"

As always, that marvelous greeting. But immediately, a confrontational kind of questioning by her.

"Want the good or the bad news first?"

Again, according to that very first lesson, the best once given, by the worst to be cancelled, swept away.

"Wait 'til I have a drink. It's been a hard day."

"Unless I'm very mistaken, you don't drink any more."

"Right you are. So let's wait anyway. Maybe someday I will again."

Expectancy. And a silence that meant he was not properly receptive to what needed to be known. However, he yielded almost at once.

"OK, go on, rip me apart. Have at me. And don't hold back any!"

"Really, why does everything have to be such a case, such a chore? Why not just take things as they come?"

"Because that's what it all turns out to be, a goddamned case of something or other. Okay, if I'm to be bothered, let's get on with it. And I really don't give a damn in what order you put it."

He was sorry even before he had stormed. She might take him more seriously than he intended or would want. "You sure know how to take the joy out of just about everything!"

"What's that got to do with what I'm supposed to be readying myself for?"

"Just my independent, humble observation. That's all."

Sometimes, like now, he didn't really mind if she baited him, made him irritable and he actually exaggerated his belligerence in order to savor it. Annoyance could be a not unpleasant switch for him, a kind of emotional gear change. If it was not the joyous kind, as he would prefer, it would at least be mobilizing enough, or antagonizing enough, to jolt him clear of his usual doldrums.

She'd become subdued. It wasn't his purpose to get her down. He needed her to be cheerful in the face of just about anything. He depended upon her for that. So he backed off and became, if only mock remorseful, at least respectfully enough measured with his words to appear contrite.

"Thank you very much, dear girl. If you don't mind, I'll take the bad news first."

"Jean is sick. She's been in New York for more than a month. It's lung cancer."

"Christ! Where's Richard?"

"Up there, with her. They've an apartment on the east side until she finishes her treatment."

"Damn, damn, damn! Those fucking cigarettes! She just wouldn't quit! Had to keep smoking her head off! Wouldn't listen! A thousand times I pleaded!"

"I think they both want to see you."

"Well, I can see them right now. From where I sit, she looks like hell and he doesn't look any better. I'll call tonight."

"Swell! That's just about swell! Is that all you're planning to do?"

She was right on him! Leave it to her to know what every situation called for. To know the proper thing and argue for it. And finally make him do what had to be done. It was yet another part of his agreeable surrender and his dependency upon her.

"And the good news? With this on the table what in hell could be the good news?"

"Nothing much. I just thought, since it's the week end, it'd be easy for you to run up and see them."

She had it all worked out. There were no alternatives. "Don't drive. Take the train."

She was right. It was right. But what prompted one to do the so-called decent or moral thing? Not, assuredly, some "higher" calling. More likely, the charitable impulses were evolved variants of basic animalistic disinclinations to go past certain crucial bounds against similar creatures displaying unmistakable signs of having been overwhelmed by an adversity. Every animal knows its special signal of defeat from those of its own species, the signal that stops the fight, aborts the pursuit. For man, a sign of helpless ness, more often than not, was apt to evoke some form of empathetic assistance. The so called "works of charity" about which religious converts were supposed to feel so good, and for which they were to be rewarded, were no more than one meager evolutionary step beyond the dis engagement of their fury by presentation of another primate's rump. It was only for reasons along those lines that he'd be moved to head north in response to the dis tress signal from his ailing old friend.

There was also the consideration, nevertheless, that the prospective loss of Jean to a savaging malignancy would be hard indeed for him to take. Already, he could imagine himself in an uncomfortable scene of condolence with Richard, her husband, after her inevitable death. But how might he himself expect to get over this enormous loss? Only to lose his wife would be a greater blow. Jean, through all the years, since they had met in college, had been his only friend and confidante. Later she became a beautiful and accomplished woman, yet was never his sexual target. Uniquely fraternal of mind still she privileged him with her secret female view of life. This made her predictable death the most terrible kind of anticipated deprivation and sorrow.

The further glue of their camaraderie was a shared intolerance for incompetence and duplicity in human affairs. But soon there would be no more late night soul baring phone calls. No snickering over the foibles of any number of conniving scoundrels. No more belittling or decrying accounts of chicanery in her commercial or his medical world. And Jean's mind, fine tuned so brilliantly by everyday experience since the London School of Economics, was now to go down in the ashes of those infernal cigarettes she could never stop grabbing for. She loved *to* hear him out on everything save his pleading that she fight this deadly addiction!

He grieved. He grieved right then and there. He wanted to weep for what was in store for her. And there was, perhaps, the faintest sensation of a watery accumulation within his right conjunctival eye sac. But this was no different from every other time. He had always been de nied the privilege of real tears, the one claimed so easily by even ordinary, undeserving, utterly unfeeling human bounders! So there'd be no release. The electroencephalographer could not cry.

Six

In the morning he had no mind for anything but the business of getting himself to Union Station and boarded. There was not even time to puzzle over the details of his tumultuous dreams of that night, which managed recurrently to disturb his sleep. Now, rather than dwell upon their subtleties and possible hidden meanings, he was satisfied to let them dissolve and fade, knowing that in short order they would be irretrievable. Good riddance to them anyway! Nothing useful, certainly, had ever come of their interpretation! Enough today just to know his dreams, like so much else, intended him no good. If he could just as easily banish what else annoyed him!

On leaving home he had chosen to take along the magazine section of the previous weekend edition of the

New York Times. During the last several days the encephalographer had been too busy with his various wanderings to settle down with any of the newspapers or magazines to which he and his wife subscribed. The three hour trip to New York stood now to be as good as any other opportunity he might come by for catching up on his reading. So, after briefly peering out a window, being swept along much too rapidly to allow of any useful grasp of what was going on in other people's rear yards, or back bedrooms, he began to flip pages.

As ever, it seemed that cheery expectations were to be realized only through the enhanced sense of self-worth to come of buying any number of extravagantly expensive and marginally useful items being advertised, page after page, in the Christmas sale offerings.

There was certainly nothing to look forward to in a report on the pollution and environmental destruction of the Florida Keys. And not much to stir one's enthusiasm, either, almost anywhere people were attempting to cope with local or international political machinations. He directed his attention, therefore, to an article which proposed to discuss, of all things, the so-called near death experience. In short order his attention was riveted to the page.

No doubt in his mind that editors published rot of this sort because the whole bloody world wanted a chance to peek into what it hoped was the next one. But that wasn't the major drift of this particular article. The electroencephalographer was prepared to abide the usual kind of nonsense about heavenly peephole experiences and their being the preview and the promise of a wonderful life to come. But this guy wrote was that because all of these purported near death experiences were so consistently pleasant, people should not be in a stew over the prospect of succumbing, or the distress possibly to be associated with transition from life to death.

Well, he considered, who the hell in his or her right mind should really care about any of that? What the electroencephalographer agonized over was not dying, but being dead! The author of the *Times* article was just one more of those innumerable prattlers, much in fad these days, to promise either that dying isn't all that painful if you just take it in stride, or that if you don't care to linger all the way to a certain end or a predictably uncomfortable death, there do exist ways, and there can even be contrived better ones, for assuring a quick and comfortable exit.

Now the electroencephalographer had settled long before this on being perfectly agreeable to dying any number of deaths as long as no one of them would actually come off. He accepted that deaths that were not sudden and unexpected were all too often reached only after protracted periods during which a person might be in pain. Nevertheless, he did not believe it would take much ingenuity, either on his part or that of carefully recruited other persons, for him to stay reasonably comfortable during such a passage, and depending on the choice of some kind of medication, be able, for the most part, to continue at his main pursuit, that of pondering his unpleasant existence. Nor was he, like Hamlet, one to brood over the threatening prospect of unpleasant after death dreams or experiences. The electroencephalographer, to the contrary, knew with an appalling certainty that death would end every thing, absolutely. What the noble Dane would want, and feared to be denied, the state of "not to be," was for the electroencephalographer the ultimate horror. To be, in any way possible, was better than that gruesome void.

As for the prospect of an unpleasantly disturbed slumber, the focus of Hamlet's concern, the electroencephalographer would be quite disposed to settle for a terminal life limited to any kind of dreaming that could be arranged for, if no more than that was manageable. He'd seen lots of people in their final comas and had not begrudged a single one of them a second of whatever it was they did with what little brain function they were still poking along on. For him, even a nightmare was better than nothing. After all, hadn't he been contending with them supremely well for years?

As for the current inclination of almost everybody to jabber on incessantly about deaths needing to be arranged for, he saw through such advocacy at once. It was no different than the ways in which people, with empty claims of being animal lovers, put their dogs and cats down un der the guise of sparing those best and loyal friends their purported final moments of pain and suffering. All they really intended was to scrimp and spare not the animal but themselves the expense and bother of caring for them any further. They were already looking to apply the money saved to the purchase of pet replacements. And even for those who actually loved their pets, and who were caught up in the sorrow of seeing them fail, euthanasia was usually the means to terminate their own, not the dumb beast's suffering. To the electroencephalographer's observation, when his own dogs, their health failing, had been permitted to die natural deaths, they did so in a quite reasonable and considerate amount of time, the only notable change in their behavior being a necessary slowing down. When they were dying, he would help with their feedings and administer what medication was needed, until they simply stiffened out and stopped breathing. If his animals ever seemed to enjoy or to appreciate what he did for them, it was when he tended to their terminal needs. But this kind of consideration for his house pets, heretofore the confidently held and usual expectation of sick people, was to the electroencephalographer's chagrin, fast disappearing under attack by the fanatical advocates of human life's surrender.

Indeed, much of what usually went on in veterinary facilities was beginning to occur in hospitals, hospices, nursing homes, and even private residences, in short al most anywhere that invalids were exposed to the peril of dependency upon others for their needs. Indoctrination to be accepting of an abdication of the right to live was fast becoming a part of the general educational process. There was no pause to remember that among the primitive tribes which practiced it, the case for euthanasia of the disabled and the old was only made on the basis of limited re sources of food and a general disadvantage for the tribe in sustaining people no longer able to contribute to the general welfare. So, they were left behind to die as victims of their own helplessness. A bit different from being put to death by relatives and doctors wanting you neatly gone, grieved over, and dispensed with, like some poor worn out house pet, so as to conserve not critical, but discretionary resources, and to get on with their own lives while avoiding any intrusive reminder of their own fragile mortality.

The electroencephalographer looked up—what purpose in reading further? The author was an absolute weirdo, a pitch man out to sell people on the joy of getting to be dead. Much better to look about him where he sat in the heaving club car, if for no reason other than to envy one fellow for pleasure being had from his scrambled eggs, or another for what satisfaction he gleaned from what his finger tracked of the ways of stocks and bonds in a copy of the *Wall Street Journal*.

Once more, he took to staring out the window, but this time to play an old game of making comparisons be tween what might be determined of the nature of things close by, jerking past him rapidly, and of distant scenes, drifting almost languidly in and out of his field of view. It was of no consequence either way. There was much more to be gained trying to figure out what was going on in his own head than what was happening out there. Besides, there was no knowing any of it. Everything seen from a distance looked better than its actuality. Pastures, inviting from afar, always came down to being arduous to cross and offered little more than humid summer heat, a variety of bugs, dirt, and what not. But before turning back inwardly to his ceaseless self study, he chose to take further stock of his fellow passengers who were also shak-ing and vibrating along with him in their run toward the city. In short order he had an idea.

Like as not, they could be evenly divided. It might be that those over to his left had the gift of faith. And those on his own side of the dividing aisle were possessed of denial. On one side minds put numbly and peacefully into limbo by the comfort of believing they were beneficently overseen. And clustered around him, the deniers, those able to close out their anxious wonderings and their fears of death either by overloading their senses or by working slavishly.

Wondrous faith and evasive denial of reality. Such absolutely marvelous assets! But where in hell had he been when mental baggage of that sort, so necessary for coping, was being handed out? Why was he not ever so favored? Having no organized religious orientation was of obvious enough origin. His parents had invoked no formalized deity. They suggested no spiritual grounds for his con duct. At home, in his early years, he noticed only that they acknowledged rather blandly the existence around the place of another presence, a friendly sort of ether. They were in the habit of calling it II god." It was all his mother and father needed to sweep them quite comfortably to ward the abyss. They would, in fact, have considered it incredible if he had ever expressed doubt regarding that mysteriously indulgent vapor. In any event, the derivation or the goodness of their II god" was something he could never bring himself to dispute in their presence. And why, conceivably, should he want to divert anyone, much less his loving parents, from an easy way through life, a way that avoided the kind of suffering he experienced almost every conscious moment and probably also during other moments of torment that weren't even within his limited powers of recall. He suspected these were out of conscious mind yet in a realm he somehow knew of. But the question remained unanswered. Why had none of their simple sort of faith managed to rub off on him?

The denial thing, however, was something else. It appeared to be intrinsic, a salutary self-preserving reflex. It provided quite inappropriate, often sustained flights of the spirit. These were not the sorts of mood elevation of the kind generated by bursts of physical exercise. Denial highs consequently were not endorphin driven. They were the effect of a peculiar kind of neuronal conspiracy operating out of special cell centers of the higher brain, bent upon implementing a kind of delusional self-hypnosis. He some times wondered if his own cellular organization of that type, as it progressed toward maturity, had possibly been disrupted by a frightening childhood experience, so revealing of the gruesome nature of existence that this evolving mechanism for self-deception could never quite get back on track. Perhaps it was one of the deaths he had learned of as a child, or some grisly scene he had come upon too abruptly, like when his usually lively classmate, the red faced Marty Ackerman, was laid out cold, immobile, and strangely gray in his plain, rough cut, sweet smelling pine box. The coffin laid across two folding chairs which sup ported it alongside that creepy looking embalmer's tank.

Or did the electroencephalographer lack denial be cause, in fact, there was a creator, but not one that worked consistently. Possibly he was even some sort of bungler, periodically turning out flawed specimens like himself, unable to ignore the fate that threatened them and there fore never getting to have what was needed for life to be tolerable. Yes, the creator, if he existed, might just be a bungler. Or something even worse could be easily imagined. Suppose the creator had really screwed up! Suppose that while experimenting with things, he had actually blown himself up into protons, electrons, and other particles of energy to cause the big bang and to create all of this strange matter floating about everywhere in the universe out of which the electroencephalographer's own flawed substance was, just by happenstance, devoid of the genetically dictated capacity for denial that others were fortunate enough to have come by. By that theory, he would be among the luckless few left to struggle on through life without the kind of genetic instruction for looking the other way, for ignoring the obviously oppressive reality, an especially human misfortune, yet a fate not actually intended for anyone by the now long-gone, possibly well-meaning, but incompetent godly predecessor.

The electroencephalographer, beset by all his doubts regarding "creation," was an easy mark for lifetime feelings of loneliness and the sense of being deserted. To be lonely lent credibility to the notion of a deliberate god that, as others had said, was now merely quite dead and gone. Or could earth, with all its life forms, be no more than the inconsequential droppings of a thing that had gone its enigmatic way, loping along through its own dimensions, not ours, of space and time, and never so much as having troubled itself to look back at the likes of odd sorts such as the electroencephalographer. Possibly, it was not only unaware of what it had brought forth, but even lacked the ability to either recall its actions or account for them! Much the same as what happens when big earth creatures walk and variously move about, ignorantly trampling upon and affecting so many other lesser living things.

Hardly could this gloomy electroencephalographer suspect there was hope for any kind of future. Just the bare sight of something dead sufficed to dispel any such foolish notion. For him there was not any offsetting way that the great finality could be ignored or its cruel, rotting nature obscured by self-deluding forecasts of a "beyond." Not even now in this especially insane season for all sorts of deliriously jolly countervailing of the fearsome awe humans carry for their individual extinction by celebrating their presumed savior's birth. There was no way out, like that, for him.

The way he saw it, less than a mere two thousand

years ago, it was a naive human brain that had elaborated and spread the myth begun by a kindly and well-meaning itinerant Jewish prophet, only to have it catch on so well there were still millions of duped human brains, brains that should know better, hungering for its realization. But which among those original ancient minds would be holding onto their same predictions of a heaven within everyone's reach, if they had managed to survive all this time and now sat both historically and factually updated alongside him in the club car as it shook its way toward New York? Would they still incline to spin yarns about virgin births, of a son of God, of heavenly ascents from a killing cross, and of eternally awaited recomings? The naive brain which conceived those myths was dead and gone shortly past the fable's birthing. Its sway should be over and done with.

It was the electroencephalographer's much chewed over opinion that modern man's anxiety-based obstinacy for rejecting the objective, his separation by time from events that were folklore, and his ever gnawing desire to live beyond limits naturally set and artificially extended about as far as could be accomplished by his science, had all together conspired to preserve his mythology. That was so to the extent that, looking about him now in the club car, he had already judged every one of those seated across the aisle from him to be variously "gifted" with some of that kind of faith.

He could well imagine, in turn, what they might have to say should they be able to read his mind. How perverse, how sacrilegious, they would declare on picking it over thoroughly! And how would he respond if all of them rose from their seats in a solid show of anger toward his heresy, heedless even of the risk of doing so at that particular moment. For now the train was hurtling so rapidly it would not be possible, however they might hold on, for achieving enough steadiness so as to allow them one clutching hand for their personal security and the other for sustained fist-shaking in his direction.

There'd be nothing but to do them all one better. "Gentlemen," he would say, "it is no heaven to which we are proceeding. After all, no heaven is attainable from hell. And that, my friends, is precisely where we are. That is where your bloody god has put us. And we are not ever to either leave this place or to stay here and suffer forever. It seems that even the likes of you and me do not deserve, or need to have the kind of punishment we now endure here daily to be extended for that long. It has been ruled to be quite sufficient for we who are here in hell to know we shall certainly die, to know that death grows ever closer and closer, and in our mind of minds or if you wish, heart of hearts, to sense, in spite of all our prayerful shenanigans, that anything for us beyond our briefly lived hell, is nonsense. Furthermore, we have all been banished to this place for something unacceptable we did in another life but shall not be permitted to remember. You see, in that way, it is not possible for us to argue about the specific injustice of it, which might distract from the purity of our suffering. No, we are here just to agonize and not to think, except about the fact that there is absolutely no way out of it. Well, my friends, how do you like them apples?"

They would topple back in their seats, the protest, the spunk, quite gone from them. A dull cast to their eyes, like dumber animals sensing the inevitable, his traveling companions would be deflated, resigned.

The electroencephalographer, however, was now upbeat. Under the pressure of having to deal with the protests of what stood to become an unruly mob in that Metroliner car, he had possibly come up with his best idea yet. That earth was in fact hell was a real brain storm! It certainly made as much sense as anything else he'd theorized over the years. And it seemed to connect vaguely with the seed of his infantile musings, the later apprehensions, and yes, it kind of came across...musically!

But then he settled down once more, made nervous by two new questions beginning to cross his mind, in their various ramifications both of them very disquieting. Was someone who thought and imagined the way he did just plain psychotic? Or if, perchance, this latest bit of break through thinking was finally right on the money, could he be in, like, some kind of danger? Though the train was warm, he shivered.

"Pennsylvania Station!"

Seven

Maybe also in other places, but certainly in New York, people seemed nasty minded, and to boot, straight out flaunted their delight in it. He was not of their kind, even though he had grown up here. His ordinary disposition was rather to confine his belligerence to purely imagined situations in which he might bring others to some kind of grief, never himself having enough spleen to actually confront or accost anyone directly. So here in New York, with passersby shoving and jostling him as they might, he did no shoving back. There was no need for it because he had, to his own mind, already acquitted himself equally well, having had it out so definitively back there with the self-satisfied believers across the train aisle. Those fellows were probably not so smugly confident any more about heaven, and earth, and where in hell that hell might truly be! The basic truth of the matter was that as he wouldn't want to take it, so he couldn't ever quite bring himself to dishing it out. Only in his odd imagining way had he ever done as much. The electroencephalographer was not only fearful of being dead, he was also, by disposition, some what cowardly in other respects.

He anticipated a very pleasant walk .all the way from Pennsylvania Station up to his favorite hotel, the Park Lane, but he was confounded now by an uncontrollable urge to look about him as he moved along Seventh Avenue to see if any details of that familiar scene were suspiciously changed from how they had previously appeared to him. It was not so. The only difference was that other faces, sensing more than accidental collisions of his gaze with theirs, sallied back with a bit more than their customary show of resentment. No, everything here in hell looked much as it had before, when it was earth. Any change was probably just minor coloration imposed by his own sensitive foreboding and the paranoid feeling his movements were being spied upon by something vengeful. This concern was quite enough, however, to convince him that henceforth he would be well advised to keep his unorthodox opinions to himself, in particular those radically discounting the conventional ways that people ordinarily viewed matters. It never managed to cross the electroencephalographer's mind, during this time of self counselling, that nary a word of anything he fancied himself to have said back there on the Metroliner, had ever actually been sounded. Strangely also, he no longer feared for his sanity. He had, at least for the time being, too far separated himself from reality to be capable of that. So he lumbered along, wondering about what might be watching or following him from behind, or perhaps even from above. He was on the lookout for any signs that what he had been up to on the train was not being well received by whomever or whatever had set this whole devilish project into motion. There was a reminiscent musicality in the sounds about, and old familiar arboreous smells upon the late morning air. Things were quite like what they had been near the beginning.

He found comfort in the businesslike manner by which the reception clerk confirmed that indeed he had made a advance reservation and then proceeded to lead him through the ritual of registration, room assignment, and credit card prepayment. It was also gratifying to see there were not any knowing side glances from that one. Also, no inscrutable behavior anywhere about the lobby. Nothing out of the usual, either, in the way his small overnight bag was swung along by the overly friendly porter. Once having admitted him to his room, that fellow proudly adjusted the air conditioning, pointed out the location of all the light switches, demonstrated how to operate phones and television, and was away, all for the sum of three dollars. Not anything more than ordinary about any of it. All very routine and calming, including the tip extraction, a maneuver he had always considered ill disguised thievery. But this time there was a tranquilizing effect even in that bit of knavery. Nothing like good old dull, reliable, expectable routine for settling oneself down and quickly rejuvenating the plod ding, workaday humors. No mystery that people found so much easy refuge in mechanical, repetitive, nonthinking behavior.

He was, in fact, shortly pleased to be back once again

to wondering about what might be happening to his mind. The return of capacity to worry over the possible impending loss of it was gratefully received. No fun at all in a paranoia that all one has left is one's paranoia! As bad as fearing a panic attack will never end, or of being unmindful of its being only a brief attack.

The electroencephalographer was now also able, for the first time since leaving home, to finally direct some attention to why he had travelled to New York in the first place. It had been his original intent to spend most of his train time thinking about his dear mortally ailing friend, but the newspaper article on the purported joys of dying had flipped him! He had been detoured from that purpose and led back to his relentless engagement of universal questions that invariably and quickly became either unanswerable or carried implications he could not fathom past certain undecipherable limits. Which left him, as usual, intellectually stalled and self-repeating half understood questions of his own making and wonderings that took him only into both new and old nonproductive blind alleys. Between that sort of thing and his imagined encounter with those seated on the other side of the aisle, he had managed to shift his attention completely away from the reason for his trip. As he reflected upon it now, it was as though this recent as well as other attempts to crack the impenetrable often wound up evolving into enigmatic dreamlike fragments, incomprehensible suppositions, originating not with him but out of something else; or they could even be taken for kinds of epileptic phenomena. He prided himself on knowing quite a bit about epilepsy, and it had occurred to him that his mental lapses might very well be epileptic fugue states or psychomotor equivalents. And of course the music thing also went well with that. People having certain kinds of epilepsy often started out by hearing music. But at this moment he seemed back on track. He was peering out the window at Central Park sprawled fifteen stories beneath him toward the north and was thinking of how best to come as gently as possible upon his old friend.

It was a stupendous view. The mud green lake twisted distantly from sight, slightly obscured by overhanging coalescent tree limbs long shorn of their autumn leaves. Seasonal defoliation was always such an ominous business, for who could ever confidently count on spring? Certainly not now, from preliminary accounts of her mediical condition, his friend Jean.

The park spread out between what could be towering cliff dwellings of the east and west side. And if that was what nondescript apartment buildings were to him, then so might the entire scene be anachronistically trans formed, but to past and future of the same moment. A considerable accomplishment! Juxtaposed imagery of ancient beginnings and expectant future. Sky vaulting modernia crawled through by ant-like human primordia. He was drawn to each illusion, yet not really inclined to the prospect of confronting either one, for this was no foolhardy capricious La Manchan. This was a fearful weighed-down fellow, quite averse to the possibility of reckless encounters at any turn, and right now, again facing up to Jean's death, the implied surrogate for his own, he was quickly out of courage for even meeting that ob ligation. So by way of a general retreat he hastened to obliterate the troublesome scene below. He Strangeloved it. Cued by an interruption in the street noise, the electroencephalographer projected a dark mushroom cloud above the city, and staged a soundless end to the park, those buildings, and all the rest of Manhattan Island. Very effective for him, that chance bit of silence. It reminded him of the old film clips of nuclear testing at Alamagordo. Just the ever-enlarging cloud, interrupted by flashes of light, and the tick of the projector. That movie about our end, "On the Beach," did it have, he wondered, a screeching bird? Was it that or was it just lapping water, or howling wind? But death was no bomb or being drained pale and cold. It was worse. It was nothing at all. For death was not something to be experienced. It was the imagined, the dreaded, endured as anticipation. Its advance notice was the realization of there being less and less life to look forward to. So provocative that vagary, because just how much less could not be known. Only someone like Jean, or a criminal facing the certain date of execution, might be able to suspect or to know the measure of that time.

How would Jean cope? There was not much to be drawn from the way she had sounded on the phone. Just her matter-of-fact reporting that she was on "chemo" and that something needed to be decided regarding a suspicious area of tumor having spread to one side of her brain. It was always hard for the electroencephalographer to understand how so many people he had known, in the same predicament as Jean, had managed to bear up and to function right through to their last consciously drawn breath.

And was the living out of lives to end as hers would end really supposed to be some kind of sacred privilege? Existence like that, however brief, was a "gift" for which to be grateful? To him the idea was outrageous. But now there was another question, one beyond whether or not, miserable or not, one hangs on to life any which way one can. Even given the little there was to be had from a life forced upon him, he was already settled on its tenacious retention. No, there was a separate question that the electroencephalographer was fielding as he rode the elevator down to the Park Lane lobby. What he was weighing was how anyone in good conscience could be involved in the process of deliberately bringing a human life into this world? For what? To realize it will lose itself? Could it be right to inflict such torment upon what one has created? Wasn't that, rather, work for a devil?

What forethought, in truth, went into this convention of life's perpetuation? Its comforts, advantages, seemed all for the procreators, not the newborn. Beyond that, the process appeared driven by a notion that the undeniability of the reproductive imperative carried implications, as well, of a moral imperative for such busy work. Revisionist rejection seemed therefore not within anybody's reason able purview. And as stringent as many might hold this "catholic" point of view, there was also, nonetheless, a popular wonderment regarding the "miracle" of life, tending all kinds of people to assign it an unassailable status not really that much at odds with the way strict Catholics embellished the phenomenon further and to an extreme. But did anyone, aside from this fellow now moving through the lobby, ever stop to think of what amount of suffering could be avoided by rejecting this death-inviting and death-dealing biological automaton called life? Had any parent, observing the awareness of life's end, as it evolved gradually in the eyes of a maturing son or daughter, ever experienced a scintilla of guilt for what they had brought about? Had misgivings for creating a being not ever truly capable of happiness because of that selfsame awareness, ever been felt by anyone?

As for human destiny, it was to do what? To orbit space as a species a bit longer, on a lump of matter ultimately to self exhaust, or to disappear along with a nearby exploding star, which the self deceivers inclined to call their very own sun? Or to accomplish, if feasible, before that catastrophe, a spread of human intelligence around the universe? That, by his measure of such a prospect's worth, was hardly for the electroencephalographer what anyone might consider a godsend for other planets. More like a bit of unfortunate intergalactic pollution with the grief of human self aware-ness. He certainly saw nothing to be fancifully considered as holy human destiny in any of it, unless holy purpose was a spread of misery until such time as all the firmament imploded once more and took the human wail along with the memory of everything else along with it.

With all of that firmly settled in his mind, it was out the front door and into Central Park South. He had but to stroll across town toward Second Avenue and East 62nd street. Jean was living there in an apartment rented from some doctor. But no more than half a block along his way he noticed an unusual brass plate attached to a building front declaring the sixteenth floor the location of a roof-top supper club called, oddly enough, the Salvation Too. What could a place, so named, be really up to? Stepping back to the curb and craning his neck, he could make out nothing at all. Even from the other side of the street he could barely see the outline of anything more than a few potted plants or perhaps some small trees along the roof edge. It might bear further investigation later in the day. There was certainly no time at present to look into it. His immediate priority was to get over to Jean's place. A quick attempt to question the doorman was non productive. The man acted as though he resented any inquiry. Pretty much wanted it understood he didn't know and didn't care what people who could afford to pay the price of being upstairs (pointing roofward) did whatever it was they did up there. Just a grudging admission of seeing, on a few occasions, around 9:30 PM or so, some black guys going up above who looked like they might be musicians. Well, no more time for any of this. The electroencephalographer quickened his pace and headed for Second Avenue.

Eight

"Is that you?"

At least the voice coming through the door was no different than usual.

"None other!"

"Just a minute, man."

That was what she had always called him, "man." Others had proper names.

"Christ, it's really a drag dealing with all these locks and chains." And finally getting it open, "What's the point to them all, anyway? For sure, no one's gonna kidnap me in this here present condition!"

There was not much to be made out in the darkness of the doorway. Just her usual tall self bending over him and the almost perfunctory touching of her lips to his cheek before she turned back again into the apartment. It had always been so much their fashion to avoid a show of affection that it could seem, to those who didn't know the depth of it, there was only a mere familiarity between them. It was just part of their way, then, when she abruptly turned her back on him and had him follow into what appeared to be a den. His first observation was that she limped badly.

The second was made the instant she came about to face him in the light and asked a much too frontal and immediate question. But that was Jean's typical directness, head-on and pointed.

"Well, what do you think?"

And incongruously, she laughed the query at him in her same old overly loud, raucous manner, but now it was so unseemly, because though the voice and the attitude were the same, Jean's great old body had disappeared.

"Why you don't look bad at all!"

"Christ, man, you better get a new set of lenses! Don't you lay that kind of shit on me, too. I get enough of it from Richard and my son Tom. This fuckin' thing is eatin' away at me. First it's in my lung, and now, it's got the shoulder and hip, and like I told you, they're even thinking somethin' in the brain."

She was truly unrecognizable. Her once appealing long blonde hair was now reduced to a few forlorn and brittle widely separated wisps she had apparently no inclination to even cover over. Below the baldness, the face was an anemic alabaster and quite obviously steroid swollen. There was not a trace of her once engagingly chiselled features.

The electroencephalographer made no further comment on how she looked. But no point in retracting what was already said. Both knew it to have been well meant but nevertheless an awkward lie. No problem, however, because these two could excuse each other just about any thing. With whom else could either of them ever manage to duplicate their perfect compatibility?

"Man, you have no idea what I've been through in just one month. First my local doc thinks, get this, it's only pneumonia! Then, when I don't get any better on antibiotics, the asshole finally sends me up here. All of a sudden, then, I've got this chest surgeon Russo who says it's lung cancer, but can't tell if it's curable unless he goes in on it. So he sends me first to a chemo guy for three weeks of some damned pre-op poison that makes me sick as a dog and knocks off all my hair. And then, when Russo finally does operate he says it isn't operable after all and fills my lung up with radioactive seeds!"

The ravaged woman sat before him, one leg thrown over the arm of her chair, apparently to ease the pain in her hip. She once again began disconcertingly to laugh. He could not tell if it was just emotional venting or the amazing show of her ability still to step back, take stock, and explode, as always, at almost every failure of things in life to measure up to what were so often her unrealistic expectations. And now, in line with that, it seemed she was laughing at the implausible notion she'd had, up until then, of being young and correspondingly healthy, reduced of a sudden to the ridiculous reality of her personal wreck age and transition to a state of decomposing flesh bristling with radioactivity.

"So now I'm having a lot of trouble breathing. They say it's due to pulmonary fibrosis. And I'm getting radio therapy just about everywhere, the lung, the hip, the shoulder, the ribs, the back. Man, you can just about name it! And you know what? From all of these guys, the chest surgeon, the medical man, the chemo fellers, and also a pulmonary gal, you know what I know? Nothing. Nothing. No fucking one of them is willing to tell me where I stand. Some shit! No?"

"I'm really not into clinical work any more, except for neuro consults and the EEG lab. But if you want, I'll make some calls and... "

"Christ no! I don't need any more doctors on my case. I've got too many of the bastards now! All I need is for one of the ones I've got to level with me. I wanta know how much time I have."

It seemed to him, from looking at her, there wasn't any at all. She changed the subject.

"And get this! How about this place? You like it? Pretty neat, no?"

To consider the question, the electroencephalographer got up and walked through the apartment. It was a very substantial five room condominium with two balconies, three baths, and marble everywhere.

"I've always said you deserve the best."

"I'm renting it from my doctor, the chemo guy."

"You're kidding!"

"First word out of his mouth is Cistplatinin. You gotta have Cistplatinin. Second is, as long as you're gonna be around here anyway, how about renting one of my apartments? I've got a beauty for you, empty and only a short walk to the hospital."

"God damn, that's some nerve!"

"That's what I thought. But then, man, I started thinking. Screw the lease thing. Who knows how long I'm gonna live anyway! I'll take it on a month to month deal. If the guy doesn't do his best by me and keep me alive he's gonna be out some nice change 'cause a swell joint like this doesn't rent so fast. Things are pretty tight right now in the luxury rental market and for something really up scale like this, forget it! It could stay empty for years."

Proud of her connivance, she started to laugh again. He'd never be able to forget how she did it. Had never heard anything quite like it. And it wasn't mere spontaneous chortle. She was intending something. It was commentary. Just before, she was cackling over the foolishness of taking anything for granted. Now it was over people being such selfish screwballs, and needing to be accommodated and outsmarted. It was her way, also, of attesting to the madness, the meaninglessness of everything.

"How's Richard handling it?"

This was a second marriage for her, but of only about a year's duration.

"Hey well, very badly, but I don't know what I'd do without him. He pretty much quit workin', got somebody to run the business, and does practically everything for me. He cooks, shops, and every day, the poor guy has to drag me back and forth to the hospital. I feel awful sorry for him. It's a bitch. Me with all of this pain, looking like hell, and you know ... "

She emitted another inappropriate laugh.

"Even though he's twenty years older than me, that man used to go off like a faucet!"

A twirl of her finger, an eyebrow arched at the ceiling, and a gasp of amazement at the measure of Richard's sexual vigor.

Nothing for awhile out of the electroencephalographer. He just sat there facing her, downcast and sensing that sooner or later she'd pick up again with what she really wanted to say.

"Look, God knows I'm crazy about him, but for Christ's sake, believe it or not, there's still lots of things out there for me to enjoy, even with all of this shit going on, and it's tough enough to hold my own self together!"

There would be more to come. She was only leading the electroencephalographer to appreciate how important she considered what would follow.

"I wanta read. I like reading. I like to look at pretty things, play with my dog. Right now, that's good enough. I can settle for it. No more than that small bit. It's all just as good as it ever was, and now considering everything, maybe even more than good."

"So?"

"I can't keep them up, my own spirits, my concentration on what it is that I like, plus play it foxy with all these crazy doctors I have to deal with, if every time I turn my back he's gonna run into the bathroom, sit on the toilet, and bawl his heart out. Man, that's just too damned fucking hard to take!"

"Where's he now?"

"I had him take a walk. Maybe he'll meet somebody nice!"

A wink, another finger twirl, and yet one more in credible laugh from the disintegrating friend. These two had never spoken about their own deaths and yet here she was prepared to live out her life in a way he'd choose for himself, given the same situation. Neither one of them inclined to think the life they'd been dealt was one to crow over, but for whatever it was worth, no point but to make the best of it.

Any privilege in it was only of somehow having stumbled on to good company for the passage. She had Richard, a son, and him. The electroencephalographer's chance fortune was limited to his wife and this friend, but the friend was preparing to die. The wife had drifted into alcoholism. Decomposition was in the air.

There persisted this expectation of a need to grieve. Back in Washington, he'd already thought about that, even tried to provoke its best and usual expression, only to be reminded of his flaw, the inability to cry. So Jean need have no concern on that score. She'd not have to demand his forbearance as well as Richard's. The catharsis of tears was denied him. At best, the electroencephalographer could only swallow hard over his mounting melancholy. There were now enough cramping throat spasms for that. But such pain, though it can distract from other hurt, doesn't relieve anything. He had no alternative but to suffer.

As they often had in the past, these two now sat silently facing one another, their purpose a privately conducted sizing up of this awful circumstance so unexpectedly and harshly foisted upon them. The electroencephalographer felt constrained to conceal his thoughts out of consideration for her limited disposition to tolerate how someone else might be affected by her illness. It was certainly no time to begin an in-depth discussion of what on some other occasion would probably have been grounds for an interesting exchange between them. Nevertheless, he was hung up now anyway, by dint of his own present needs, on the whys and wherefores of the human requirement to cry.

He found himself remembering oddly that years before

this there had actually been a failed attempt to mount a musical on Broadway called "Cry For Us All." As best he could recall, it was based on a story or play by O'Casey, something about "Hogan's Goat" and being "Lost In The Stars" or whatever. How it all came about was not really that important. He was pleased to remember, though, in spite of his lousy mood at the moment, that the show featured his favorite musical singing star-the beautiful Joan Diener. Well, it had been an extraordinary production, but it folded, nevertheless, after a run of only one week. Probably, he had always considered, because investors could hardly be attracted to the idea that anything about crying, and particularly for the whole bloody world, would stir Broadway crowds to plunk down their hard earned money at the box office. Imagine being asked to come to Broadway by an appeal to cry, and to do it to music yet! Besides, crying was not only unmanly, it was downright un-American!

But also he seemed to recall a report from *Mans Health* that the average man actually had occasion to cry once a month. For whatever it was worth, women, on average, cried once a week. He was about to chew that a bit further, for its full implication, when she broke the glum silence.

"You got any ideas?"

It was a no-nonsense question, framed in a way of indicating, somewhat sternly, that his response to her query was to be practical, down-to-earth. No maudlin sentiment would be acceptable, nor was it called for. It certainly would not be brooked. He was being summoned to attention and out of his self-absorption.

"Well, I've always got ideas, problem is there are usually too damned many of them, and they're often not very clear or doable. I don't know but that you have any real options save to go along with the doctors. They're supposed to be qualified people, aren't they?"

"Well man, there's always options, different ways of doing just about everything. And I've got problems, big problems with going along with these guys."

"Like what?"

"Like two days ago I had this spell where my right hand started to shake and my speech got kind of slurry. So they lined me up with still another doctor, a neurosurgeon. This one orders a CAT scan of my head, takes no more than one peek at it and says there's something maybe starting to grow on the left side of the brain. It's all kind of vague, but for sure he seems to see a hell of a lot of swelling there, and get this, no operation! I'm no candidate for surgery upstairs either."

"So?"

"So? So we're into doing nothin' at all to stop it from gettin' bigger! Isn't that a bitch? But because the thing is making me epileptic, he gave me medication to maybe keep me from having any more spells. But no guarantees, man, nobody promises you anything! And I get other stuff to bring the swelling down."

"Steroids."

"Right."

"And?"

"And? I just told you, and nothing, not a god damned thing! Christ, that's the fucking problem! The big, big problem! The number one problem! No one wants to do anything at all, except for maybe some more of the chemo stuff. For what? To make me more anemic? For more transfusions? So I can get more infections? I already had two of those. And hell, I don't have any more hair that's left to come out! But get this. On this chemo deal nothing definite. I may, mind you I may, get to receive the chemo, but only if I'm lucky enough so they decide to fit me into some kind of program, a research program, like what they call an approved protocol! I gotta somehow manage to be so lucky? Man, these guys are weird! I'm ready for just about anything, but have a heart fellas! This is something else, it's really something else!"

The electroencephalographer was quite ready to cry. He damned well needed to cry. No problem for him to appreciate why good old considerate and loving Richard had to spend so much time in the john. No risk of it happening, though. Jean was assured of that. What other men were reported to do once a month, and Richard now seemed to do almost continuously, had been beyond his reach the entire forty-six years of his existence. He thought about his incapacity in that department and was then disturbed to have another statistic suddenly intrude. Soon he was hating, absolutely hating the fact that in this dread fully charged up situation he still chanced also to remember that on average, men had intercourse 2.55 times per week! Why? Why in hell should some data like that have the appalling effrontery to insert itself, barge in and just about desecrate this scene? Was his mind that uncontrollable? Could it be, though, that all minds operated in the same fashion, but only he fretted over it?

As far back as his first day in the EEG laboratory he had marvelled over the relentless night-and-day insistence of the brain to churn out its electrical currents, making all of those tall, slowly undulating wave forms and fast moving low voltage shudderings. The electricity never stopped for a moment and only changed a little bit from night to day. The brain and the mind within it were always at work, never really suspended. It seemed to the electroencephalographer that all anyone harboring a brain ever did was tune in to it occasionally, kind of check it out for what it was up to at the moment, and see what it was making of what it had been fed by the special senses. It had its own program of busy work, unless asked to focus on some thing, and like some malfunctioning computer it could also, on its own, erupt unpredictably into consciousness, spewing out what might seem a total irrelevancy for the moment at hand, as it was doing now. This was more than awkward, it was very bad timing indeed for presentation of a dumb statistic on human sexuality.

Or was it that everything that happened in the mind was at base really irrelevant to everything else; that all seeming relationships were impossible to ground in actualities? That all of experience was nothing more than what the charged-up, gelatinous convolutions within our skulls are stirred to concoct within the eternally restricted limits of happenstance and an unpredictable brain circuitry. Awareness forever imperfect, an untrue representation of what is. And that should be some kind of a clue as to who or what was involving all of us in this bizarre game!

His composure belying none of this animated but secret pursuit of that riddle, it being shared as usual only with an unseen other party, an undefined listener, Jean saw only the face of the electroencephalographer's friendly concern and pressed on in a voice astonishingly steadfast in light of her obviously escalating fragmentation and decay.

"I've got to have something more than this! I'm a goddamned candidate for something better than this! I know what I know, know what I have to do. And you should be able to guess it. Figure it out!"

"Christ, Jean, how can I put myself in your shoes?"

"Because we're all in the same god-damned shoes sooner or later. There's nothing special about me, just that I'm there now. Look, all I've got, all that anybody's got is what we can make of things with our brains for whatever time there is."

It was a chillingly faithful recitation of his own exact thoughts of the moment. Were they that alike? Or were these two brains somehow transmitting back and forth to one another from across the room? Were they duplicates of one another or electrically connected?

"You think that for whatever time I've got, I'm gonna go along with these jerky doctors of mine? You think I'm gonna just sit back and let this thing eat its way through the most important thing I've got going for me, what I'm all about, my brain, my mind? Bull shit! I'm taking off! I don't care what they say!"

"Where the hell you going?"

"Man, this crazy lady is no fool! I've been doing my homework. Out in California there's this guy with what they call a gamma knife. It's like from Sweden. You lay down on the table, they locate the tumor with still another CAT scan and zap, one single supervoltage shot focussed from all around and that's either the end of the tumor or it's stopped, at least for the time being, dead in its tracks."

"What do your own doctors say about that?"

"They're opposed. Even the ones that never heard of this stuff and don't know anything about it; they're opposed. One son-of-a-bitch actually sat down and wrote me a letter saying if I go for it he's off my case and relieving himself of all responsibility for the consequences! The bastards want

I should just stay here and take a chance on maybe having them poison me with more of the chemo. They don't fool me, man! Not one bit! What I really suspect is if I should go off and do my own thing, sort of tailor my treatment to what I damned well need, it'd be a breach of some stupid research protocol they've got me listed under. Then man, when I croak, they won't be able to claim my results for whatever experimental project I'm probably logged into. Well, they can forget it! I'm already scheduled for California. There's birds, and bees, and flowers, and dogs, and books, and even without the sex thing, which you know I was always great for too, there's still things for this old brain of mine to work on. Out of my way, old buddy, gimpy leg and all, I'll trample you under if you try to line up with all these creepy doctors wanting to keep me from saving this beat-up mush of mine. I mean to have it working for me, man, right up to the fucking end."

And the irrepressible spirit of his dying, wasting, friend chose once more to express itself in a burst of self proclamatory, defiant laughter.

"Jean, you're something else. I've got to hand it to you. You've got it all figured out just about right."

"Hey man, we're all either dead or dying. But getting it like you say, right, that's the only way. And you know what a control person I am. I have to call every shot down to the last one. Gotta maneuver, gotta mastermind it, 'til I'm out of any more calls. Layin' in bed, not able to talk or to catch on, maybe also being paralyzed, that's my worst nightmare. So if this guy out in California can keep me mentally intact, right up to the last, I'm for it. Besides, I've got arrangements to consider. Need to think them through. Got to do some providing, for both Richard and Tom."

The year before, the electroencephalographer had talked to her often and through long hours during the dragged-out fatal illness of her brother. He, an alcoholic, had been run down on the street and died finally of head injuries, unable to be saved by surgery. Jean's reaction of that time was recalled now by the electroencephalographer. It had not been the pragmatic approach she was presently mustering for her own illness. During the weeks after her brother's death she would speak of his mysterious presence, particularly at night when she walked out of doors. The sense of her brother's persistence was so strong she considered it the possible sign of death's impermanence. Back then, those star-fed, wishful inclinations of hers had made him uncomfortable. But now he wished his ordinarily levelheaded friend every conceivable delusion.

They sat quietly together, nothing more of consequence remaining to be said. Their business was concluded and afternoon shadows were darkening an already gloomy room.

"Keep me posted," was his gentle admonition on parting.

"Watch yourself, I worry about you," was her cautioning.

Nine

It wasn't said as part of the conventional banter of routine leave-taking. She meant it, and her solicitude did not sit well with him. That she, who should have no concerns but to milk what few rewarding moments she could from life, would still take time to concern herself over his well-being was an embarrassment. Walking south along Madison Avenue, the electroencephalographer couldn't understand precisely why his sensitivity for this was so keen. After all, the regard they had for one another was long-standing and strong. So why did her expression of it even under these trying circumstances, make him so exceedingly uncomfortable? It was hard to tell.

When he had left her apartment, he had no destination in mind, other than the Park Lane Hotel, nor was he under pressure to get back there at any particular hour. This left him free to just move slowly down Madison Avenue with ample time to observe each person, irrespective of their wishes. Hardly any of them looked different from those back home in Washington, save for that peculiarity of New Yorkers, previously noted on his arrival, of returning his exploratory glances with conspicuously more hostility than in other places he'd been. This was a trait that did not change with the season and was certainly not affected by a yuletide, presumed at that very moment, to be overflowing with good will. That hostility, moreover, probably had nothing to do with problems regarding street crime or other deteriorating conditions of urban safety, drugs, or assorted social pestilences. The New York look, in fact, was just about the same wherever one chose to stroll, be it Harlem or lower chic Madison Avenue. No, the possibility for being looked at this meanly as the prelude to some kind of physical accosting or other criminal abuse of one's person was not cause for the phenomenon. Nor was it because the Prince of Peace, yuletide or no yuletide, had somehow decided to give up on this place. There were, in fact, here in New York, many more decorative acknowledgements of his approaching birthday, and especially along Madison Avenue, than the electroencephalographer had seen back in Washington, where the confrontational return stare was of a notably lower order of intensity and incidence. Possibly it had some thing to do with the crowding factor. People did need space, and it could just be they were more jammed together in New York than in Washington. That idea didn't seem to really catch on with him either. It would have to be looked at, anyway, with reliable numbers in hand regarding population density as against the specific levels of observed hostility in different places, or maybe it was just a chance evolved characteristic having some survival advantage on the New York scene and had been passed along generation to generation by people who had somehow acquired the gene for such mean streaks a long time ago for reasons that could not possibly be identified at present. By the time he got to 55th Street, and in spite of innumerable opportunities to study those hostile stares both at close hand and from more safe distances, his final conclusion was that, as for so many other matters, he still had no satisfactory explanation for them.

He proceeded west toward Fifth Avenue, bothered by the fact there were now two things he could not under stand. There was the matter of his perplexity over Jean's concern for him and also this business of the unaccountably nastier New York stare. So preoccupied was he by all of this, he scarcely noticed that he had suddenly come upon one of his old haunts. Whether he found himself turning in automatically from force of old habit or because of new needs based upon a lot of things among which was a sense of being hounded just a little bit too much by all of that unpleasant eyeballing going on out in the street, was not a question he'd be able to answer either.

It was the St. Regis Hotel, and he was not moving left through the lobby because St. Regis was the resident patron saint, whose favor or advice he sought. Rather, it was because a little further along in that direction lay the King Cole bar, and there above the bar, however the general decor might change from year to year, was an enormous well-preserved painting of that merry royal person him self, surrounded by all of his courtiers. It was also, to his mind, the most superb bar could possibly be encountered, and where, when he used to sample, and better yet that could drink them, there were concocted the world's very best martinis, among the few things he'd once inclined to consider truly glorious. Old habits don't really die at all, and surely not when an electroencephalographer becomes severely stressed out. For these reasons, circumstance con spired to have him abandon his oath of abstinence, and soon he was sipping at and allowing to slither under and over his increasingly beguiled tongue the most exquisite of all martinis in its perfectly iced form.

He had never really considered Old King Cole to be that all soulfully merry, whatever his attributed reputation. Staring up at him now, the electroencephalographer saw the same person he'd become familiar with during all of those years he'd been stopping by to admire him. This particular king was actually more sly than merry, and he sported the half smirk, half sneer that was the mark of the kind of realistic, skeptical royal who took his pleasure, by and large, from observations on the prevailing state of world idiocy. Otherwise, the electroencephalographer would never have been inclined to visit Cole's court for the sampling of his kind of wisdom. A Solomon, the elec-troencephalographer could do without. Solomon was too much the simplistic preacher of a self-satisfied morality and held people at their respectful distances. Cole, on the other hand, was like a good old drinking buddy who had just about everyone and everything figured out and who wouldn't mind letting you cozy up to him. Raise a glass with Cole and it was amazing how an annoying mental constipation could suddenly be relieved. Every once and awhile in former days, to get himself over such an impasse, the electroencephalographer would drink with Cole, or if in some distant place and under the same requirement, would have him still in mind on the occasion of such alcoholic unblocking.

Now, as the electroencephalographer continued to sip his drink and was experiencing a mounting internal warmth along with the subtle first advance hint of the giggling kind of euphoria, it appeared to him that today there was a ruefulness to Cole's half smirk. And that he was more into deploring something rather than sneering over it with that other part of his expression. No question about it! The electroencephalographer was being reproached. For what? So unlike Cole to hold someone to a moral or any other kind of standard. What was it that he was supposed to be feeling guilty about?

Well now, this was quite a first! After all, today's situation called for no commentary from Cole on this particular visit. He came by chance or habit or for convenience, not by need of his usual kind of audience. And yet here was Cole choosing to insinuate something disparaging regarding a matter for which the electroencephalographer had nary a clue, much less had posed a question. What was he to do now, sit there imagining for which of his actions, recent or even remote, that very discernible bit of disagree able peering down upon him, was perchance appropriate? It was like being given the key, go find the lock! He was certain, martini or no martini, Cole's response was being ventured before any query had ever been put to him!

Cole, in general up until then, a fellow of the same mind as he, had unexpectedly chosen to make him feel that somewhere along the line he'd not met some sort of obligation and was, for lack of any other good word for it, guilty of something. It was not a pleasant situation, especially considering the fact his mood today was already in a free-fall. The electroencephalographer had always held guilt to be a feeling of very inconsiderable priority and also somewhat low-brow, albeit still much in vogue these days for defaulting on so-called "moral" commitments. These, he thought to have freed himself of. Any reminder he remained accountable and sensitive to something like that was unsettling at the very least, and at the worst raised serious questions as to the true extent of his behavioral emancipation. He thought he had schooled himself to conform in his behavior with what was correct only in the purely biological sense. That was as much concession as he'd want to make in matters of social civility. Some body else's ground rules were not to be acceptable and were not to bind him. He was not to be bothered about some failure to meet standards others set for themselves or presumptuously expected of him.

But now he could see that the guilt business was not fully rooted out of him, and he wondered if he would ever really succeed in killing it off. That concern, however, had to be set aside for the moment because the question currently on the table was much more pressing. To whit, what action or lack of it, ordinarily connected in the general behavioral milieu with feelings of guilt, was unfortunately triggering these unpleasant sensations in him? And why did Cole look so reproachful? It had to be something very serious if someone like Cole, ordinarily cynically inclined, was brought by it to making common cause with the moral majority! The electroencephalographer deliberated intently over it. He sipped more deeply into his martini. In no time at all his glass was dry.

About halfway through a second, when in spite of himself he was starting to get fairly jolly, he wondered how neat it would be to always feel better than his usual self, something on the order of how he was getting to feel right now. Of course he knew he was rapidly becoming drunk, but that didn't mean he couldn't simultaneously field any number of serious questions! And yet the tentative consideration of still some other of his vexations served only to remind him of that nagging, unresolved, original question. Yes now, but what was it again? He hadn't a prayer. He was baffled. It eluded him! The couple at the table to his rear, toward whom he turned unsteadily for advice on the matter, looked startled but didn't seem to know either. He focussed back on Cole and as he did so he knew both the question and what was being questioned instantly. Yes, yes, his selfishness! That was the issue. Such conduct on his part was certainly not escaping of the electroencephalographer's awareness almost from its inception. It had been troublesome to him as far back as when he was made uncomfortable by a childhood tendency to covet what others enjoyed or owned. He was a very selfish child. He had even envied his poor parents for their pathetically meager personal possessions. He could recall his self-reproach and disgust on begrudging his father, for the little he had, including a small but tidy wardrobe of business suits that the modest hard working man took such pride in. He envied just about everybody for something, even for the way so many of them, adults and other children alike, had time to waste on inconsequential activities whereas he would hold himself to a rigidly self-imposed discipline of schoolwork and study. Why, now, for the very first time, should all of that business be unexpectedly dredged up for review? And why was it he always felt bad when he acted selfishly? But why think about that today? It could not conceivably be a selfish thing to stand there by himself at the King Cole bar. He certainly couldn't have invited Jean along, not in her condition. Besides which, he hadn't even known he was headed here. And as for his wife, was it wrong to have left her at home by herself? Not in the least. He knew her well enough to be certain she'd have turned down any invitation to New York. And the last thing in the world she had need of was cocktails at the King Cole or any other bar.

Ah yes, his wife. He could certainly manage to think of other ways, real ways of his having been selfish about her. It wasn't right, for example, to regard her simply as his good fortune, like a kind of asset, someone to relish and depend upon. But that's how it was with her or any one else he inclined to care for, but not about. The test of really caring about someone was assuring they suffered no deprivation, even when possible, of life itself, but for their sakes and not his own. It shamed him to know he could not meet that standard. If others happened to benefit from his attentions, even thrive upon them, it was so he, not they, might feel or be the better for it.

Ordinarily, the electroencephalographer's remorseful hesitations were as infrequent and transient as any other inclination to fault himself. Today was different. It was as if the combined effects of that particular mix of gin, vermouth, King Cole derision, and what lingered of the earlier sense of embarrassment on leaving Jean's apartment, had conspired to virtually obsess him with the issue of his limited capacity to care about other human beings. The electroencephalographer then chanced to dwell on his friend Jean as the kind of person who acted more in line with conventional morality. From that he was led to know exactly why their earlier parting had been so bewildering. It was only because she had chosen to express at that time the kind of caring he himself was not capable of. And he was even the more mortified by her willingness to expend on it the very limited resources of time and energy she now had left to her. Thus his guilty frame of mind.

Well, that was one question no longer unanswered, and one mystery resolved! The problem now was that the martini's liberating and euphoric effect upon the frontal lobes of his brain had become undone by all of this serious and revelatory self-analysis, and he began to fear there was no will left in him to take even a feeble stab at being in halfway decent spirits over the next few hours. All he had accomplished was to become unsteady of foot and concerned that to drink any more would only exaggerate his inclination to brood. Again life had given, only to take away.

But why should he be so hard on himself? Didn't everything that lived and breathed, when you got right down to it, act primarily out of self interest? Wasn't that the biologically dictated, genetically encoded, survival oriented, and evolutionarily dictated (all favorite expressions of his) way to successful being? Yes, but now human life was supposed to yield to consensus and group concerns, the general welfare depending on the well being of each individual. Unfeeling or incompletely feeling societies were assumed to fail. The current hype was for altruism.

And what about this guilt thing, the sense of shame for not being able to conduct one's affairs that way? He thought that, like everything else, it was just hit upon by chance, handed out fortuitously by nature, and then carried along because only guilt for not acting in accordance with concern for others could assure and advance a cooperative venture, giving it an advantage over less enlightened competition in the wild. Well, this time at least, he'd been there to get part of the package! Result? He might from time to time feel like some Saint Sebastian painfully arrowed not by Romans but by guilt, yet be unable to change his devious conduct however it provoked remorseful second thoughts.

For in the beginning, there was guilt. And it was observed to be good. But then it took it upon itself to divide into two parts, guilt with a purpose and guilt like his, devoid of purpose. That is to say, there was at first original guilt. No doubt about that. Didn't everything have to start out original somewhere? No?

The electroencephalographer looked up from his now empty second martini glass wondering, one: should he have a third at the risk of collapsing onto the floor and possibly also into a direful, perhaps bottomless depression, and, two: where in the hell did Cole stand on all of this? There was no telling. Cole was now sporting a smug, self-satisfied leer, and looking off into the distance while one of his jesters whispered some kind of amusement into his left ear. Those two might even be joking at the electroencephalographer's expense! It dawned upon him that Cole might have transmuted over the many years since last visited, in line perhaps with all of the redecorating and renovating that had been going on at the hotel. The St. Regis ownership had changed hands and it was now part of a hotel chain hellbent on tearing apart much of the old majesty of the place. His Highness was beginning to look to him like no more than an uncaring provocateur, retained and hired to keep things at the bar in a more modern day kind of stew, having lost any old-time interest he may have had for the nitty-gritty of down-to-earth serious cogitation. The sort of thing that went on there before all of this updating business got started. So it looked as if the electroencephalographer would have to take it from here, entirely on his own.

Back to original guilt. Well, original guilt had happened to follow, as he was just starting to think, what was also the trend for living substance, that is protoplasm, at the time. It had divided. But divided into what? Seemed to him he had just worked that out, no? The electroencephalographer stared down into the third martini and tried to overcome his now fractured certainty for anything. One, divided into what? And two, who in the hell ordered this one?

"It's on the house, sir. Our compliments. Please keep your money! No consideration!"

Could really turn out, in fact, to be no consideration, he speculated, should he come to fall flat on his face! Well, he didn't have to drink it. It could just sit there on the gorgeously polished mahogany and provide excuse for his hanging on in the place. He'd leave it right where it was, with its scrupulously well chosen, fleshy green olive resting on the bottom. This self-same martini glass was an other classic, chilled ideally, the moisture of the atmosphere condensing on its surface and starting to trickle down along the stem, over the base, and ever so slightly onto the gleaming mahogany. Well, he couldn't have that happen! So he tidied up with a napkin, moved the glass a well chosen distance to his right, and turned his attention instead to a bowl of pretzels as well as back to the theory that guilt had hit upon the principle of binary fission and under gone, not a biologically customary division into two exact duplicates of itself, but rather into two quite different things entirely. For now, he remembered, there had come unto being from original guilt, the guilt that was post facto observational (without purpose) and the guilt that was anticipatory (purposeful). How did the electroencephalographer come to know this? Easy, he had only one kind and none of the other! He could always tell when he had acted poorly and always felt badly afterward for having done so. But he was never able to know beforehand that this adverse emotional result was to be anticipated. He had been deprived of anticipatory guilt! It was always something with him. No gift of faith! No denial! And when guilt was being passed around, he now concluded he had received only half the favor, observational but not anticipatory guilt! He was a truly deprived person, and perhaps for just that reason forced to habits of inquiry of extreme, to the point of queerly aspiring objectivity.

It was now seven in the evening, and on Saturday nights the King Cole Bar, always a popular rendezvous for both New Yorkers and out-of-towners, as well as emigres like himself, was getting crowded. Although a few tables remained empty off to one side, there was no more room at the bar. It was tighter than elbow to elbow, and people were either reaching over him for drinks or reduced to standing sideways. The electroencephalographer, regarding himself as a kind of honored alumnus of Cole's place, held steadfastly to what space he considered befitting a veteran patron. Planted at the bar with both elbows spaced widely apart and with head hanging a bit forward and to the left of his martini, as he supposed himself to have carefully placed it, he noticed it was gone!

"Somebody took my drink!"

"Sir, you drank it."

"The hell you say!"

"I beg your pardon, sir, but that's correct, and since it was your third, I thought it not proper to offer you another."

"I want my drink! Someone's poached it! Christ, I don't know how you can keep an eye on all of these monkeys anyway! And it looks to me like they've all got four or five arms, the way everybody's grabbing for the damned bar!"

"Are you seeing double, sir?"

"Don't get smart with me! I'm an old timer here! You know that?"

"Are you driving tonight, sir?"

The bartender was evidently taking the matter of a possible fourth martini under very serious advisement.

"I'm not drinking! I mean not driving! And I'm sure as hell not flying yet either, so give me my goddamned drink!"

"Just a moment, sir. One second while I serve these people."

And what exactly, wondered the electroencephalographer, was he supposed to be, suddenly not a person?

The bartender moved a few feet away and occupied himself with other patrons. It seemed to the electroencephalographer that he was stalling. At least he had the dis tinct impression that when this dispenser of perfect martinis next held his silver shaker overhead in the service of those other customers, he was being unduly slow, almost theatrical about it. Then, a minute later, there was the feel of a hand pressing down upon his left shoulder. In New York, no telling what that might mean, but for sure, if it was what he thought it was, someone right behind him needed quick discouragement.

"Sir?"

It was no such thing. And taking stock of the guy, he decided this interloper was definitely not someone needing to be straightened out. Also, as fed up as the electroencephalographer might feel for all of his being respectfully "sirred" about this evening, as well as for the utterly unforgivable lifting of his martini, this particular bit of "sirring" required his attention because it was out the mouth of a very large man wearing a small official looking button pinned to his lapel, and having slung over his shoulder a portable telephone with which he could probably summon just about anyone.

The electroencephalographer had never actually encountered a security person of this particular sort before, but he knew about him from various sources as well as from the movies. The man and he spoke briefly to one another and struck what under the circumstances was the only deal possible. It was all very discreetly arranged for. Probably enough so that when it might later be thought back on, the electroencephalographer could still consider this to be his special place. Anyway, in just a few minutes he was seated comfortably in the lobby. He had been given, by what turned out after all to be a very nice if strict fellow, a splendid tapestried chair upon which he could spend whatever time was necessary before deciding where next to head himself.

After about fifteen unproductive minutes of such contemplation, during which he noted the demeanor of newly arriving guests to be peculiarly cheerful and utterly out of keeping with prevailing trends as best he knew them, and after deciding that perhaps things somehow got that way on Saturday nights, which he wouldn't know about because he always stayed home on Saturdays, he stood up and left through the revolving door, of a mind to just cast himself, so to speak, upon the waters, or the street, or whatever, on chance that something interesting might come of it. And as for old King Cole, well right now they could very well do without one another

Ten

It was cold standing outside even though the St. Regis marquee was underslung with infra red heaters as an accommodation to guests awaiting transportation. As soon as the frigid air hit him, the electroencephalographer also realized that he was getting hungry, and well he should be, for he had not really eaten since having breakfast back in Washington. Where to dine should be easily decided. North up Fifth Avenue was the Plaza Oak Room but directly opposite, facing the Regis, the Cote Basque might be a bet ter choice. For some reason it seemed to beckon. Probably only because it was the closer. And it was a good thing that it did so since the electroencephalographer was beginning to consider the strong possibility he had in fact gotten to finish that third martini. Not only was he very hungry, but he was more than just a trifle off with his balance. What a less scientifically inclined fellow would call "tipsy." So the closer restaurant was definitely the better choice.

"Cab, sir?"

"I've had enough of all this sir crap, if you don't mind!"

"Beg your pardon?"

"For what?"

"Something wrong, sir?"

"There you all go again!"

"Merry Christmas to you too, sir. Please, if you don't mind there's a gentleman waiting behind you."

"And what the hell do you think I am?"

The doorman, appreciating there was not much to come of this kind of dialogue, opened the door of an idling cab in such a way as to provide entry to the man who waited and simultaneous eastward displacement of the electroencephalographer, whom obviously, by now he considered no gentleman at all, or at least no more of the sort to be wanted outside the Regis than had been determined desirable inside the King Cole Bar. Christmas or no Christmas, things were getting to be downright inhospitable right there in what the electroencephalographer regarded to have once been his favorite haunt.

Having made the Cote Basque his next destination, and now being eased away by the Regis doorman, it was a simple if staggering matter to abide the momentum of both his intention and commenced motion and proceed in the direction of the discreetly canopied restaurant across the street. He had the presence of mind, however, to cross 55th Street enough farther east of the Regis so that he could come back westward upon the restaurant with enough wind in his sail to allow reasonably steady but sneaky enough progress up to its doorway from the side rather than to risk staggering directly upon it from across 55th Street. This was the case because yet another door man lurked curbside over at the Cote Basque, and there was no point in being challenged or having to pass some kind of sobriety test as the price of gaining entry to the restaurant. Things were coming to a pretty pass here in his favored part of town. Almost seemed like no one knew these were hard times and patronage like his could make a real difference. Make or break, that sort of thing.

This doorman, on the other hand, for all the electro-encephalographer's apprehension, seemed to have the un-canny ability to pass him inside and yet at the same time entirely ignore him. Aware of the slight, he entered deter mined not to trouble himself over it. He'd roll with all of these inconsiderate punches. New Yorkers were, after all, a strange lot!

While checking his coat, the electroencephalographer chanced to wonder, by way of noting the helter-skelter and somewhat precipitous manner in which he now proceeded, if in fact it was really true that he who hesitated was lost, or was it rather more likely that he who hesitated was the only one apt to find himself saved. He recalled reading commentary regarding the intrinsic temptation, the irre-sistible draw for charging ahead when the better wisdom would be to stay put. The issue was not to be pur sued further because he was being encountered by the maitre d'.

"Well, here I am again!" he announced with a grin. "Do you have a reservation, sir?" as to a complete stranger.

This could be unbearable after awhile. What exactly

was all of this substitute for honest name calling supposed to accomplish?

"Would you like my real name?"

"Not unless you have a reservation, sir. We're quite full up for the evening, sir."

"Now look here, there's not but three tables occupied and I'm only after a quick bite. I'd sure appreciate if you could accommodate me. I used to eat here, you know, all the time!"

The electroencephalographer slipped the man a surreptitious fast ten.

"Are we alone this evening, sir?"

"Just you and me."

"I mean, are you expecting to be joined by others?"

"Nope. What you see is all you get."

"If you'll have a seat at the bar, I'll see what can be arranged."

"Terrific."

No more martinis. Definitely, no more martinis. In fact there was a better drink, one just perfect for the occasion. Not exactly what the doctor might order, but still right enough anyway. It was just he and another bartender. No one else around.

"I'll have a black coffee, but let's splash it with a little Remy Martin."

Amazing, thought the electroencephalographer. He hadn't done anything like this in years. No question though, he remembered exactly how to go about it. Just what the rest of "it" stood to be, however, was not so easy to figure out. Nothing to do but just play along and see where this unpredictable scenario was leading. But something, very definitely something, was afoot. After all, he'd no more than stepped in out of the cold for a drink on his way back to the Park Lane and look at what was happening! It seemed too that his evening was unfolding in an uncanny way, maybe even being choreographed by someone.

Why was it that he seemed never, absolutely never, alone? It was as if his every thought, every one of his moves, was being somehow witnessed. Personal privacy always eluded him. That was not to say (and perish any slip of his tongue on it for fear of being taken as an out right nut) that some kind of unseen being was on to what he thought or did. But secretly, he did feel that way. Just for once, the electroencephalographer thought, wouldn't it be nice not to be doing things or puzzling over various matters for that other presence's consideration?

The wall behind the bar, at which he was seated alone (save for this invisible other one) was papered over with what looked to be a harbor scene at Villefranche. No people were represented in it. But in spite of this solitude, sitting by himself at the bar with his Remy and coffee, with the deserted waterfront cafes frozen in time to the wall above him, he continued to feel observed. Possibly, all this sense of a spooky kind of togetherness really lay in the fact that to think meant verbalizing, however silently, and there was no way out of sort of hearing one's own internalized speech. So when thinking, one was in essence talking to oneself. And for any kind of talk, even of this kind, it might be that the brain automatically assumed there would have to be a listener. And if there was a listener, one could not consider oneself alone. As simple as that! It was all worked out to his satisfaction! Right there on the Cote Basque bar while he sipped the black coffee tasting also of the Remy

Martin, he'd resolved something that had al ways puzzled him. But would it follow then that other animals, those not having speech, were therefore blessed with a kind of solitude no human could ever know, bedeviled as all humans are by this everlasting thinking, talking, thinking business! Probably so. In fact, doubly blessed they were, the other animals, as in their true aloneness, they comprehended nothing either, about the inevitability of death.

There he was, back to that, to death. Some roads might very well lead to Villefranche. You could not take that away from them, but they, nonetheless, like all the rest, led not only also to Rome but to death as well, or at least as far as the intoxicated electroencephalographer was concerned they did, since for him, everything, wherever it stopped along the way, most concernedly, eventually, wound up graveside. So he was back on a morbid track once more and wondering how he had ever made light of anything in this dreadful world. Because often, he did manage to joke around, to laugh, to toy with flippancy. At times he could even be the absolute clown. What was all of that about? Not certainly to enliven anyone else. Probably, like laughter itself, nothing but a cheap grab for comic relief. It was to suggest alarming but only imaginary extremes, to no end other than a happily guaranteed escape begetting the solace known as laughter, where laughter could be sibling to disburdening tears. Well, but once again he bitterly re membered he couldn't do that sort of thing, that is cry. Maybe that was why he sometimes horsed around, played the kidder, the needling provocateur. He must do some thing, after all, to break from his misfortune of knowing death so well, and although he'd much prefer to cry, he couldn't evoke that complex of self-comforting reflexes: the muscular, the lachrymal, the cerebral. It was not within his power to do so. He appeared forever denied the tearful kind of comfort, that advantage claimed so easily by others only brushed by death yet refused to him who lived with death more than with life. Not that he did the other thing, the comedy, that well, but at least by his slapstick or wit, inept as it might be, he had managed some respite.

He thought, though, if only he might have the unknowing aloneness of the other animals, he'd forego his clumsy humor, at best a self-deceptive pleasure, for the trading. It would be so much better not, as they did not, to grasp the black reality than to lack the ability to cope with it reasonably by crying and have to settle for this incongruous business of comedy. One good cry over what actually was, would be worth a million inappropriate laughs for what was not. Yes, to be lucky like the other animals, and fearful only of what their simple senses in formed them would be his preference. No point to be knowing of anything more. Even to be bored as animals might be, was fine. The rub lay in being smart enough to know what bored one. To comprehend or suspect what any trouble or pain was all about!

The problem, again, was in thinking, that tedium endured by human minds sentenced to labor over the significance of appearances. A mischievous assignment that, or worse. Because for him there was no ultimate significance to anything, and as it had first come to him on the Metroliner, the torment of being and of knowing (that is thinking) might have been intended. So much for the "gift" of mind! Better to see and to know nothing but the simplest significances!

To test what that might be like, the electroencephalographer started to fix his gaze in various directions, all the while blocking every inclination to make appraisal of what he saw. The bartender, for example, became no more than a certain configuration of form, texture, movement, color. He had no age, no sex, no attitude, no unpleasant body odor, no dislikes, no salary, no scheme for getting people to order more drinks, no anticipation of a tip, no wife, no family, no girlfriend, no nationality. He did not allow himself to consider any of these ordinary conjectures or attributes in respect of the bartender. He was no more than the image of the bartender, or rather, the image of what was seen when he looked in the direction of what, for someone else, might be interpreted as being a bartender. By and large, his response to that was not at all neutral. It was pleasant! That image, devoid of values, was pleasant! It had shapes and colors, symmetries and asymmetries, of themselves possible of being related to in an affectually positive way. So too, with the harbor scene at Villefranche. He just took it quite happily for what on its surface it appeared to be, and not as representational of anything at all. In a few minutes more he was working his unbiased scrutiny upon a two-something visual pattern (young couple), just off to his right and stationed (seated), at a geometric dark shape (table), with slightly different kinds of feeling, but still of a type not all that bad either.

"Monsieur? Monsieur?"

He would prefer that this new image, neither chosen by him nor invited, but suddenly now hovering before him, would desist from emitting unwanted noises which he was finding it difficult to keep separate from their significances, although it was pleasurable and comforting to be able to localize those same sounds to the region of a variably opening cavity ringed by vermillion something or other, and having individual white cuboidal structures just within its margins. He therefore, and quite brusquely, waved it aside with annoyance.

"Monsieur! I have prepared your table!" Again he waved it away.

"Monsieur!"

The devil, it was the maitre d', now of a mind to address him in French, as a way, he supposed, of making amends for that earlier challenge to his right of entry onto the premises. He had no choice but to suspend his investigations and to follow along after him. The fellow had appropriated his specially enlivened coffee with his right hand and was flourishing grandly with the left in the direction of a table situated against the wall. There was no option other than to get himself seated there, but all the same, the electroencephalographer had to endure the frustration of being interrupted, just as he was getting onto something extraordinary. It would appear that he could, if and when he chose, be just like all the other animals, sort of go on vacation from himself, and get quite a kick out of it, to boot. In fact, it might very well have been better to stay hungry and continue with something like that. He might have preferred to remain as he was, apart from any immediate reality, like an empty headed dreamer on the verge of awakening but still finding pleasure in vacuous drowsiness. So too did the electroencephalographer try to hold on to his new state of mind and fight off the maitre d's intrusion into it, although but fifteen minutes earlier he was practically begging the man for a table like the one he was being led to now.

"Will this be satisfactory, monsieur?"

"No problem."

"Would monsieur like another drink from the bar?"

"I'll just look at the wine list along with the menu, thank you."

The electroencephalographer, with those items soon in hand, did not confine his attention to them. He could not possibly do so, because seated at an adjoining table was a most remarkable appearing woman, perhaps twenty five years old. Hers was an angelic face, of complexion so delicate and pure it needed no cosmetic enhancement. With no flaws, the face could have no inherent sensuality either, the woman drawing it rather from a provocatively formed body and audacious black silk clinging tightly just about everywhere one could want to see female incitements to male arousal. From the shoulder-length fall of her soft brown hair to her impatient, seductively fidgeting ankle, the woman was a study in the anguish made possible by female come-ons.

"Has monsieur had time to decide?"

"Don't bother me."

"Pardon?"

"I'm sorry. I'll have the Medoc, number thirty-four, along with the smoked eel. How's the Dover sole?"

"Superb, monsieur. And how would you want it pre pared?"

"Just grilled on the bone, please."

"An excellent choice. Would monsieur prefer the wine at once?"

"Please."

Always seemed to him they resented it when he ordered red wine along with a fish course in these snooty upmarket places, but what the hell, except for Montrachet, he didn't much favor the whites, and besides, he'd just seen an article attributing longevity among the French to their experience with red table wine, but not with the white stuff. So at least on something, the world affirmed a personal leaning. And also, any more of the pale kind of alcohol, based on old experience, would give him an awful headache before the night was over.

Back to the wondrous one, but now she was up to something quite unsettling. She had leaned well forward across her table and was reaching beyond it in order to run her right index finger down the left cheek and along the upper lip of the man sitting opposite her. Until she had moved in that fellow's direction, the electroencephalographer had not even noticed her companion. He was too fascinated by the splendor of the woman's appearance to pay any attention to the man. But upon her reaching for him in that way, it was a natural matter for the electroencephalographer to wonder as to who might be so exceedingly lucky as to merit her attentions. And that was occasion and reason for his instant astonishment and revulsion. The damned guy had a frayed collar, rumpled suit, and as much hair growing out his nose as his ears! How could she possibly spend her time with such a person, and how could the man discredit her so by looking as he did? The. arrogance, the presumption, of the bounder! But also the terrible judgment of the woman! What could be her purpose? All too easy for someone like her to have almost any man. As for the unkempt one, under the circumstance, what would be wrong about it if someone, any one, even he the electroencephalographer, tossed him the hell out of there? It was enough to ruin a person's appetite!

"Is there something not right with your eel, sir?"

"No. Is there something wrong with yours?"

"But you are not eating."

"How the hell can I? Look at what's going on over there!"

"But they are so much in love! N'est ce pas?"

"Have you taken a good look at that guy?"

"Ah yes, but monsieur, is not love blind?"

"Maybe, but you have to smell things too! Hard to believe l'amour conquers all, no matter which way the wind happens to be blowing."

"Ah, but monsieur is perhaps the comedian?"

"No, monsieur is failing to see anything at all funny about it. Monsieur is dead serious, and monsieur is also in love and having an erection, if you must know!"

"Bon appetit, I must go now."

The Medoc was superb. The electroencephalographer had started by savoring it, but soon he was nervously through half the bottle, even before finishing his smoked eel. Just as the Dover sole arrived, the disheveled man got up, presumably heading for the men's room. At that moment the electroencephalographer saw also that the woman's napkin had fallen to the floor. He hesitated only until her companion was out of sight before seizing upon that opportunity to bolt from his chair and fairly catapult himself across the aisle separating their two tables.

"I think this must be yours,"

"Oh my! Thank you so much." The beauty reached out to recover her napkin from him.

"No! no!" withholding it from her perfect person. "You must have another."

Stretching across to an empty table he deftly borrowed a fresh one from there, and with a flourish, snapped it across a lap enviable by every conceivable measure. It was all done with quick precision as part of an operation that also included his tossing of the contaminated napkin onto a nearby serving tray.

"You're very kind."

She looked at him without the trace of a smile. It was unbearably exciting.

"I want to take you for a carriage ride!"

"What?"

"I want to take you for a carriage ride!"

An odd idea. And he hadn't a clue as to how in hell it had come to him, particularly since it was freezing cold outside. But who was to say how any ideas originated? If that's what he seemed wanting to do, then that, for what ever the strangeness or obscurity of the reason, was what he quite obviously needed to be about with this woman.

"That's impossible!"

"Look, it may be crazy, but impossible it is definitely not. You just think about it. I'm going to be right over there for at least another hour. And listen, it doesn't have to be right away. It could be tomorrow!" When the electroencephalographer got back to his own table he could see that things at hers were no longer as before. With the man's return their conversation seemed to become more matter-of-fact, and there were no more caresses. It was as if their relationship had become strained. Every once and awhile the young woman's gaze turned in the electroencephalographer's direction and he was tempted to think it was inquiringly, as if in effort to figure him out. Not a sign, though, of her imparting to her companion what had passed between them. She was obviously keeping it to herself, which meant that just that quickly, they, although separated by years, several feet, and total ignorance of one another, were joined, possibly forever, at least by one small secret.

It made him remember how long before this, while attending a concert with his wife, he had felt quite abruptly the pressure of a foot, the foot of a woman seated on his other side, against his own. He recalled that way back then, upon advancing his own perhaps a millimeter, there was from her a response no bolder, but still detectable. It went on that way through an entire symphony, and when during intermission, she, accompanied by her husband, happened to cross paths with him in the lobby, their eyes met only for an instant. That glance of hers was designed to be vacant to him, but what it revealed, nonetheless, was the void in her life. She lived well and in an obviously decorous but yet longing way. What had been between them and was to be resumed during the rest of the concert, was just the pathetic scaled-down substitute for what the woman wanted. In a harsher age the husband might have been dealt with, or circumvented, and she would have been consumed. These, had thought the electroencephalographer, were supposed to be better times, when although that's how we really still incline to think and act, we are supposed not to. Provoked by his recollection of that ancient episode he did scant justice to the Dover sole, but drank more of the red wine, and stared now not at the young woman's beautiful face, but at her ankle and her foot, and at a shoe not too different from that other one, back then, of the concert hall.

It had not escaped his notice he had been drinking heavily this evening, a former habit he had given up for several years. Also, that at this inebriated moment, and particularly since sighting the woman, in spite of the gloomy circumstances of his afternoon and the dutiful purpose of the trip to New York, thoughts of death and the catastrophe of non-being were no longer capable of intruding upon an utterly unheralded air of well-being and light-spiritedness. Even when they crossed his mind, dismal reflections were no longer capable of lingering and causing emotional havoc. They could no longer sabotage his mood. Marvelous, he thought, the way alcohol, almost as surely as a surgeon's knife, managed to sever, if only temporarily, access of the recently evolved, second-thinking and prudishly restraint-oriented frontal lobes to the hell-raising, charged up centers of the ancient brain, and also to weaken their resolve. Alcohol provided occasion for even someone like himself, the electroencephalographer, to either revel or rage, depending upon what his circuitry happened to be up to at the moment by numbing all the connections between those two brain regions.

From the time his blood alcohol level hit .134 and he found himself under the seductive influence of silky femininity, soft brown hair, and that inviting inversion of a well turned ankle, death thoughts couldn't get at him. They were unable to bridge this chemical barrier operating against them, or to recruit the troublesome attitudes ordinarily plaguing him. Pleased with his new mood, the electroencephalographer drained the remaining wine from the bottle and ordered another Remy Martin, this time with out the coffee. His now deliberate purpose was to set his meddlesome frontal lobes completely adrift. He aspired to float himself even further and euphorically free of them. In vino veritas? No! In vino a quick escape from veritas! For now life was inappropriately good, feelings were good, and the world was a place of wonderful, possibly everlasting, expectancy. And as for the probability of a hangover, of sweats, tremors, cloudy thinking, in the morning? Who could care about tomorrow when his evening was becoming impossibly erotic, when it was suddenly what every thing should really be all about? When one could sit and stare at that face and at that ankle!

"L' addition monsieur?"

"Add up? Nothing's quite adding up to anything. All it comes to is one helluva big frustration!"

"Pardon?"

"I can't leave, maybe can't even live without her. I'm in love. Don't you see that?"

He was still sober enough to know he should not be pointing so obviously at the woman.

"One must be practical, n'est ce pas?"

"O.K. I'll have the lemon sorbet."

She was the one, that right girl he'd given up on ever finding. She was that "ideal" girl Maurice Chevalier used to sing about longingly but feared would somehow "pass him by." She was that girl, whom as a youth he could only hope existed, and had to be patiently awaited. Yet back then he had wondered, if it was going to really happen, might he somehow have an inkling of her identity a bit sooner, or even a hint as to her whereabouts? How could he have known it was not to be because she was not yet born? But now she was sitting right across from him and there was no wife back home. There was no dying friend, no rendezvous with death, no spirit spying upon him. He was a pining youth once more, but in a state of infatuation and sexual arousal over a real person, not some damned fantasy.

The woman ate, rarely speaking. The man never said anything further. He kept looking at his watch. Perhaps they were going to the theater. Or, because they were at a table which could seat four persons, might they be waiting for others to join them? No, it was probably too late in the evening for that. Then quite precipitously, the man asked for his check. But she was still eating! Almost as soon as the maitre d' brought it to him, the strange fellow, now clearly in a·hurry, pulled three bills from his wallet, rose from the table, leaned over to kiss the woman upon her cheek and was gone! Mind bogglingly, everlastingly, gone! He had unbelievably departed! The electroencephalographer's heart forgot to beat, then it pounded at his chest wall. His mouth became dry. It was the same as being, all at once, alone with the desired. Something else was also happening deep within his mid-abdomen, because what he had only joked over with the maitre d' was now a miraculous possibility. The electroencephalographer's hopes, his pulse, and much more than that, were all on the rise.

What he could not have anticipated also, and there was no question of it being the case, was that the woman began to fix him with a persistent stare of her own. He toyed with his sorbet, fingered his glass of cognac, glanced about the room now filling with other diners, but she, eating, sipping at her own wine, kept her eyes dead on him. It was a maddening but wonderful turn-about.

All he had to do now, if ever he was right about anything, was to walk a few feet and take her for his own! Who could figure that the endlessly repeated wishful day dreams of his adolescence should finally and actually come to pass this way? It would take no more than some simple, clumsy, sweet-talk of the kind he had fancied and practiced endlessly in his teens, while lying in bed at night, before sleep would put the damper on his imaginary overtures to girls and women of all kinds and ages, each and all succumbing wordlessly and invariably to his advances. Now all of that could actually come about! What trembling excitement! What joy!

But no, she was getting up to leave and his heart was bouncing about, not only at risk of skipping beats, but of arresting in one fierce final spasm. He must catch up with her! It could not be permitted to happen! He jumped from his seat. And then, wonder of wonders, saw that she was turning toward his table and in a few short steps was facing him.

Eleven

She reached out and touched him. She had touched him! It was somewhere on his left arm.

"I'll just say good night. You have yourself a nice carriage ride."

Then she smiled. No, not a smile. Why, she was beaming! It was the radiance of life bursting to excess. The glory of death cast out! There was no room in him for any kind of feeling but of how great it was to be alive, and especially like this, with her. He was carried much beyond the easement of depression by the connivance of some self-prescribed sexual nostrum or slyly calculated program for promotion of his libido. No half-baked remedy this, or something to be analyzed, picked over. This was for real! "Nice? It can't be nice unless you come along. And don't say it's impossible. Look, sit down, please sit down and let's at least talk it over. It will be quite something, even if all we wind up doing is no more than talk about it." And he was thrilled to see her do it. She was sitting down with him, and even more than just smiling broadly! Now she was laughing, laughing in an unembarrassed, unrestrained, almost raucous, but just correctly short of uproarious, way. No question about it, she was genuinely finding the electroencephalographer to be amusing.

"You've probably had too much to drink."

"No argument there, but the booze has nothing to do with it!"

"Well what has it to do with?"

"I've never seen anyone like you. That's the pure and simple of it. You know, I used to imagine one day I'd find the girl and the occasion for saying something like that, but it never managed to happen, and now here you are! But even if I never had occasion to think about it or wish for it or to anticipate such good fortune, and kind of re hearse it, I would have spoken anyway, just as I have. I look at your face, the way you move, your hair, and now there's the smell of you, and I can't help myself. There's no possibility of anything but to react this way, to find you absolutely adorable!"

"And you're a nut! But maybe a nut who could turn a girl's head!"

"I can't really do that unless you like me, at least a little."

"Well, right now all I'm thinking is you're either crazy or drunk or both."

"There's got to be something else or you wouldn't have me being the lucky one and sitting here in front of you.

You know damned well I'm truly smitten, don't you?" The electroencephalographer could feel his ears be ginning to redden. Embarrassment for his emboldened way with the woman had finally overtaken him. Sober or drunk, he had never before been this outspoken by way of admiring anyone. That was something he had not believed it possible for him to do. But now, finally presented with the supremely appropriate occasion for it, he was determined to act on the conviction that this sudden good fortune was not apt to come his way again and to seize his moment. He slid his hand across the table and rested it firmly upon the woman's forearm. It was a solemnly conducted move and what with the serious intent of the gesture, as well as his vulnerability, vouched for so obviously by the flushed appearance of his face, the woman was moved. She responded by turning her forearm outward and drawing it back just far enough to appose her hand to his. They sat silently, staring mostly at their entwined fingers, as if to puzzle over what that entanglement might mean. Soon, by some decision simultaneously arrived at, fingers and palms moved hesitatingly, then persistently, against each other. No more explicit signal was needed to indicate her tentativeness had given way to agreement for proceeding further. The electroencephalographer had a question.

"That fellow?"

"Married, and no big deal anymore. It's over. You?"

"Also married. Here on personal business. Just about dead, and wanting, at least for awhile, to forget it. I could do that with you."

"You sick or something?"

"Hell no! At least not as far as I know. It's just a matter of my finally catching on to the absurdity of appearances."

"The what?"

"Nothing is like it seems, and what there is, is doomed. Only feelings are real. They count, and communications too, but not necessarily the content of communications. A tough thing to realize when life is more than half over and you've not either had or shared much in the way of good feelings, or bothered to establish any intimate lines of communication. Things have tended to get a bit grim lately, what with the foreboding, the slow slipping away, the imminent prospect of nonexistence, for a mind that hasn't ever really revelled in anything, but nevertheless one wanting still and desperately so, a continuum for its awareness."

"Wow! You some kind of shrink?"

"No. I'm in neurology and neurophysiology. I actually work in EEG, the interpretation of brain waves."

"High powered stuff, right?"

"Not at all. As a matter of fact most of us can master just about anything. You know, it's a toss of the dice, as to who does what I do, who picks up the garbage, who fixes vacuum cleaners."

"So?"

"So sweet girl, if I'm lucky enough to live a little longer I'll be able, someday, maybe to think back on to night and how great it was to have a moment in time with a beautiful woman I felt nutty about in an absolutely spontaneous way, with no second thoughts, she being no compromise on something possibly better and to be awaited, but being rather the certain one, the real McCoy, the one and only. Get it?"

"OK, I'm game. I guess you're safe enough. We'll just

see how it goes and if I am your kind of girl, for a couple of hours, anyway. We start with the carriage ride, right?"

"Precisely."

Now quite overwhelmed by all of this unexpected acquiescence, he had the sensation of a tremor as he helped her on with her coat, a soft, dark, furry thing, just slightly darker than her hair. And yet there were no really overt signs of his excitement. The electroencephalographer's hands were inspired to move in a steady, deliberate manner. Once outside and into 55th Street it amazed him how natural it was to immediately put his arm around her waist so as to draw her hip against his own as they walked into a brisk wind toward the Plaza Hotel and the carriage drop at the corner of Fifth and Central Park South. How could he possibly even know how to do this? He had never done it before. Of course he'd seen other couples walk like that, but it was not by way of any recollection he had found his way to it. It occurred reflexly, instantly, like so many other actions that are just right. And he could never have imagined what enormous pleasure would come of it, as their forward progress was made by thighs and hips jostling or gliding over and past one another. Each step was a sensual reward, until at the northeast corner of Fifth, just beyond the Cote Basque and not in the dark, but in the open and directly under a blazing street light, he had no recourse but to stop, twist about, and draw the woman to him in a determined, crushing embrace.

"Whoa there, I can't breathe!"

But all the same she was laughing warmly in an exultant deeply throaty manner.

"Breathe later!"

And the electroencephalographer and the mirthful

woman kissed, not passionately, but delicately, lips scarcely touching, then broke it off as if on cue, only to nudge brow against brow, press cheek upon cheek. It was a silently, softly conducted acknowledgement. Somehow, by the absurdity of chance, circumstances were such that these two fit. Before crossing Fifth Avenue they paused to hold one another at arm's length, size each other up, the electroencephalographer fiercely expressioned, the woman her green eyes moist, but still laughing.

"Hey, don't you ever lighten up?"

She swiveled her head from side to side, and widening her eyes, advanced upon him. The electroencephalographer bent forward boring his forehead into hers, attempting a communion of depths he had always considered separated by the barriers of surfaces and the limits upon words.

"It's so difficult to be close, really close to someone, almost to bond. I've never managed it, but here I am feeling, all of a sudden, for the first time, that I might just be able to carry it off with you, and yet I don't know a damned thing about you! It seems to be happening, and not be cause we think alike-I don't know what you think about anything-or because you're beautiful. I've met other hand some women. But it's happening because of an instinct that's never taken hold of me before but is sure as hell grabbing at my insides now. This is not to be trivialized, either, as what they say can happen on very first sighting. It's as if I'm locked into the very sound of your footsteps."

"Hey, remember? I thought we were going to have us some fun!"

For the first time in a long while the electroencephalographer laughed also. Then, he grabbed her by the hand

and hurried across Fifth Avenue, pulling her along behind him.

"Take it easy, buster, these are high heels! Oh look, isn't that awful?"

A squirrel had been run down in the roadway. Only its hind part remained. The hide of the unfortunate animal was reflected inside out and rearward, to expose a red pulpy mash of lower trunk musculature still attached to the partially covered inert and sprawling hind limbs. The electroencephalographer paused to have his kind of say. "At least we're spared the sight of his death mask."

"It's awful all the same!" They hurried on.

"Right. But the pain is in it's being about us, and not about it, that thing, that half an animal back there relegated to the damned gutter."

The electroencephalographer continued to rush her along, yielding only scant consideration for her high heels, and at the same time determined to further his point.

"That's the reason you were repelled by what you saw. There's a message in it, and it's all about people, not about squirrels. Only one difference between us and what's left of that poor beast. It's that, although we all wind up the same way, we humans still think our lot is different. It stems from a self-centered orientation, and not in the reality of anything at all. As soon as we human beings began to figure a few things out, we got the cockeyed notion that just for having that ability we were something special. Well we're not, we're just another kind of animal."

The woman pulled back and mockingly took a defiant stand, chin upturned and jutting forward to support her strong disagreement.

"Speak for yourself, brother. If you want to be squirrely, be squirrely! Me, I'm a person, and a damned nice one too!"

The electroencephalographer bent forward to kiss her anew but stopped short of it.

"Your eyes are green, aren't they? My mother had green eyes."

"How'd you ever manage to notice?"

"Notice yours? Why, all I do is stare at you."

"No, silly man. Your mother's. Where did you ever find time to notice your mother's eyes, what with all the monkeys, and cows, and of course so many squirrels after equal time!"

Now she did have to be kissed again, and this time passionately. How else to respond to someone this endearing? It was, all the same, a bit disturbing. There were so many unanswered questions. Who was this gorgeous woman with whom he seemed uncontrollably infatuated? What kind of person, would, after such slight consideration, take off with him, a complete stranger? Why did he have the feeling she was so perfectly suited to him, and his wife back home in Washington, was not? Also, the thought intruded once more that this was how things

occurred if they were fantasized or happened in adolescent dreams, not in adult life. But he was not either day or night dreaming at present. And, bolt out of the blue, why now such luck, since neither miracles nor strokes of good fortune had ever been part of his experience? On a different note, he wondered if because of his dreary obsessive preoccupation with death, it could well be he had simply fallen instinctively into a childish behavioral pattern, if only to evade a further deepening of his mood sufficient to weaken his resolve for going on. Was this present escapade with the woman just some automatic mechanism like that, a physiological intervention for his self preservation? Being a bit drunk, the electroencephalographer could speculate no better than this, but was still astute enough to grasp the incontestable fact that whatever might be his own motivation, conscious or otherwise, to embroil him self as now he was doing, he could not act alone in this matter. He was assuming responsibilities as a partner in a match of sorts, and was not only finding it to be an indeed charming obligation, but also discovering he was not very likely to be permitted any opportunity to reverse himself and to shirk it.

"The carriage ride! Do we or don't we?" she demanded, escaping from his embrace.

"We do. We most certainly do. You were not brought this far under a false pretense. Sweetheart, your carriage is waiting for you right over there. In fact there are two of them, and you get to choose."

"You do it. I don't know anything about horses, or carriages either!"

Nor did the electroencephalographer. He only remembered that they seemed to be always lined up in front of the Plaza Hotel whenever he happened to pass it by, and he would often wonder what it would be like to ride through the park that way, given the right circumstance. Now that he had been presented with one, to be heading for the carriage drop was no more, no less, than natural. What point, in any event, to making an issue of the choice? Both steeds appeared, at first sight, to be sound enough, and it wasn't as though he was intending anything arduous for horse, carriage, or driver. What he had in mind was to settle snugly under blankets with his lovely new found friend, inhale the cool and clear night air along with her perfume, and suspend the bothersome thinking pro cess. The horse could just about hobble along on its knees for all he cared! A resumption of mindlessness was to be brought about. Something on the order of what was interrupted back in the restaurant while he was waiting at the bar, but needing to be started up again now in her most supportive presence. Besides, he was beginning to get the idea of having to be more circumspect about floating opinions on arguable matters. She, and probably rightly so, appeared to have no patience for it. After all, his complicated whys and wherefores weren't really part of their arrangement. So no point to being anything but laid back and accommodating. What she meant to him was only about loving and thereby possibly retrieving what may have once, a long ways back, been genial, harmonious, and yes ... perhaps musical.

The electroencephalographer was reaching back for something vaguely remembered and possibly beyond recall. He wasn't even sure there ever were any such elusive events, presumably forgotten, but responsible for the recurring musical sounds. But the beautiful woman could possibly be a break through for getting him by and central to what had been, up to then, only certain outer ripples apparently stirred up by something in his past. To date he had made no progress toward the source of those sounds.

This was his new chance. As he saw it, the living world (and also much of what is inanimate) progresses through time, changes, and reproduces, primarily by the process of pairings. According to his reasoning, a certain order of integrity had to prevail for the unions to be successful, like the perfect fusion of equal positive and negative charges. So, possessed now of a female person, on all obvious counts the ideal other half for his particular kind of conjugal pairing, he might very well stand to do somewhat better at making headway with his probing. His evolving idea, now, was to start afresh in his search, with her in tow, and from out of that condition of mindlessness he had only this very night also had the good fortune to stumble upon. But it had to be done covertly. Accordingly, as soon as the old man in battered silk topper hawked the two of them aboard and the carriage began to roll through the park, he set him self right to it. That is, he drew back under a comforter, held the woman in his arms, and reclining upon a pillow, turned her face into the side of his neck, allowing his mind no more liberty than to pulsatingly register the erratic beck-oning of the stars above them, and the hesitant light of the street lamps getting intermittently by the intervening trees.

She interrupted his return to mindlessness. "Do you mind if I live?"

"Did you say something?"

"Well, the only other person is topside and so far the horse isn't saying very much!"

"What was it you said?"

"Nothing very important. It was only, once again, about my right to breathe. I was losing it! You had my face buried! Also, not much to see that way. You do get out of touch, don't you?"

"Sorry about that. Sometimes my attention does tend to wander. I'm back now."

He knew very well he had not merely set his mind to roaming. The electroencephalographer was trying to squelch it altogether, at least for a little while, so as to instigate what he hoped would be something revelatory. That project had now to go on hold because the woman required his undivided attention. She had turned away, hand to chin, elbow and side pressed against the carriage seat back, and was peering into his face, engrossed by it. Her legs, curled up under her, were partly exposed, the comforter having fallen to the floor of the carriage.

"Look, I'm satisfied you're harmless, but you know, so far, that's just about the extent of it."

"The rest doesn't count? What I think of you?"

"Hell no! Men are always chasing after me! I imagined that by now we'd be having us a good time."

"What do you suggest?"

"Man, it's your carriage ride, but I'd of thought you'd at least be talking about the sights or something, and not just be falling back and clamming up on me! And don't start on how close we really are to horses! Besides which, I'm quite able to appreciate this one's rear end without any help from you!"

"I'm awfully sorry."

He took both her hands and kissed them, gratified to see she was still smiling and responsive, despite her protestation.

"Like, what do you say about those stars up there? I did catch you ogling them."

Good. He knew what was required.

"Well, we call them stars, but actually they are mostly suns much like our own. There are billions, maybe trillions of them, and they are so far away that the light they send our way takes millions of years to reach us, so what we are really seeing from stars is only the light of distant suns, and a light that started out in this direction when all we had here on earth were dinosaurs and other reptiles."

"You're starting up again!"

"OK. OK. Let just say the stars are twinkling for no one but you and me."

"Now you're getting there!"

"And as a matter of fact, the whole thing, what we are doing here right now was intended that many million years ago, to the extent that everything was put into motion that far back so that just at the right moment you would be here, I would be here, and the light of all those suns would also arrive at exactly this romantic and magical moment."

"See what you can do once you try!"

"And not only that, but between those billions of stars, which are actually suns, it isn't really dark at all. That is an illusion created by our being blocked from the light of our own sun by the earth's rotation, keeping us kind of in the shadows, where that star-born light reaches out to us from as far as it does. But out there everything is really, optimistically and gloriously bright, and so it should be, because all of creation is wonderful, including you, me, and that horse's rear end!"

"Had to spoil it, didn't you?"

"How does that spoil it? Besides, nothing can spoil this. That's what it's all about. A billion years ago we were predetermined and predestined to enjoy one another."

"You wanna bet?"

"But sweetheart, what could be more perfect than this?"

'Tm bouncing around the park, legs freezing cold, with a married guy who is out there somewhere in left field most of the time, and you're telling me that's gonna be a perfect relationship?"

Now that she had called his attention to them, the electroencephalographer was thrilled to see, frozen or not, besides the ankles he was so taken by earlier in the evening, there were legs of equally substantial quality. He reached down to retrieve the comforter which had fallen away and drew it back over her, leaving his hand to rest against her left thigh until impelled to squeeze it and then to slide his hand further down to rub and stroke her calves, it all being done as if to hasten her rewarming. Then, shifting over to grasp the inner aspect of her other thigh, that closest to him, he held it firmly, the while kissing her with much abandon, to the extent that on finally breaking his tongue away from hers, he made a point of clashing their lower teeth together. Why, exactly, he chose to consummate the kiss in exactly that fashion he had no idea. It simply seemed the right thing to do at the time. One could consider it a sort of primordial reflex. Except in the matter of the toothy apposition, the woman returned his attentions in kind, and so much so there was no doubt at all about his arousal. Also no question but that she had full grasp of it.

"Sure it's perfect," was a much moved electroencephalographer's reply.

"While I have you, mister, mind telling me how old you are?"

"Forty-six."

"My God, you're up there with my father!"

"Well now, your father would have to be that old to qualify for his wonderful privilege of being your dad. But as for me, my particular age is only what's required to still be alive and inclined to kick a little. And sweetheart, if that's what I go for right now, I owe it all to you! You've inspired me!"

"Just so you know, I've never gone to bed with any one your age."

"Bed?"

The electroencephalographer was startled, both by her directness and the raising so quickly of a prospect he'd not entirely taken for granted, at least not so soon.

"Yes bed, the sack! Where in hell you think we're headed, the Museum of Natural History? If that's where you've got this dumb carriage pointed you can let me out right now and I'll just walk myself home from here!"

"But how could I be that lucky?"

"To have me split?"

"No dummy, to go to bed with someone like you, and all so fast?"

"Well, let's not say it's because it's written in the stars, or because you've fallen in with a hooker, either. I'm no such thing. It's just because somehow we've gotten our selves into this situation where now we have the hots for each other and there's no point in letting it all go to waste."

"You want to go to my hotel?"

"Where's that?"

"The Park Lane."

"It's a lot closer than my place, so go for it, unless you absolutely must have more of this clip clop stuff."

"No! No! Not at all! Driver! Drop us at the Park Lane!" Well, this was indeed a twist. The electroencephalographer still wanted, above all things, to live, but now suddenly it was for no more than long enough to get them back to his hotel room. There, beside this fantastic creature, he could die if need be, in peace. He was, in fact, half tempted to confess to her that morbid measure of his enamored condition but thought better of it. She might not be impressed.

Might even be turned off again by his kinds of fixation. So he just pressed against her without saying anything further, one hand to the back of her head, the other exploring her breast, and the kissing became even deeper. It did not skip his attention or his marvelling, how ever, that the death fear, entirely consistent with all of his past observations, was put entirely out of mind by his surging libido. Of course he'd appreciated that phenomenon for some time. It was the basis for his periodic trysting back in Washington. But what he was not prepared for (and this was what was so different and astonishing) was that here in the circumstance of intense sexual longing, one with which he was not that familiar, the fear of death was not only out of mind, it was irrelevant to any consideration. The only thing that counted was to get this woman to the Park Lane as quickly as possible.

Twelve

The driver balked at his proffered reward for a thirty minute incursion into Central Park.

"What's this supposed to be?"

"A ten."

"You gotta be kiddin', mister! I get thirty-five. Where you been?"

"Sorry about that. First time out in one of these things.

"Enjoyed it though!"

"So I noticed. Thanks. Well, have a nice night you two!"

The electroencephalographer, having pulled more money from his wallet and paid the man off, hurried into the hotel, once again hastening the young woman along behind him. He slowed his steps, however, while crossing the crowded lobby, and drew her closer to him, encircling her waist much as he had done during their brief walk earlier.

"You got a problem?" she asked, noticing their change of pace.

"No. It's just a swell chance to show you off. I'm a very lucky guy and don't mind being envied for it."

"You're also a weirdo! Let's get the hell upstairs!" She took his elbow and jerked him towards the elevator. It was so flattering. No girl, much less such a bedazzling one, had ever shown this kind of enthusiasm for going to bed with him. He could only exult. Although there were other people on board the lift, he pulled her to him again, surrounding her, not only with his arms but also managing somehow to get a leg behind her. She was just about smothered and still another kiss lasted all the way up to the fifteenth floor.

The electroencephalographer's behavior was no mere bit of exhibitionism aimed at other people on that elevator. What he might say or do at this juncture was governed entirely by his condition of extreme arousal. Already for several minutes, he had been surprised to experience a degree of dull discomfort associated with his distended state and an amount of early urethral discharge, quite novel for him. Accordingly, he had none of his customary self control and was hardly aware of anything at all, save for the beautiful woman. Now his hands really did tremble as he advanced the room key towards the latch. "Need some help?"

"It's not my fault you're so damned luscious! Okay, you do it!"

He watched admiringly. Having taken the key from him, in little more than one facile movement, she had the door unlocked and swung back, and had stepped into the room, tossing the key rather grandly onto a nearby chair. Heading toward the bed, she peeled off her coat and then her dress, letting them drop to the floor behind her. But turning around, she discovered him to be still standing and gawking, in the opened doorway.

"Are you coming too? Or are you the porter? No? Well, let me guess. I know! You're just hung up there so I can have a little light from the hall to undress by. Dearie, it's not really necessary! We have all kinds of working lamps in here and if push comes to shove, I can even strip down in the dark!"

"Sorry. I'm finding all this a little disorienting."

The woman pulled him inside by the lapel and closed the door behind him. Then she helped as he in turn began to undress. While unfastening his shirt, she drew his head down and kissed him. It was done, he thought, fondly.

"No need to be disoriented, lover. All you have to remember is where I am."

"Christ, how could I ever lose track of that!"

Quickly they finished undressing and groped for one another. It was as if, under urgent need to fondle, squeeze, tongue, and somehow caress so many secret places, at long last once and for all, he could find something out. Next to bed where they had no prerogative for delaying passion's insistence any further. There was no time even for turning back the covers. For the electroencephalographer it was a union that worked so well it could in no way be considered, either then or later, just a lucky break. The declarative words "intended" and "right" were sounding. And they had a ring to them much like the old, oft repeated music. At the end, there was not in fact, a true ending.

Breathing hard, perspiring, even though having fulfilled his obligation for both of them, he was surprised there wasn't the usual sense of satisfaction. He still wanted her, possibly more than ever.

"You may be old, but I'll say this for you. You don't play old."

"I wasn't playing!"

"Now, don't be a drag. Let's ease up on that kind of stuff, at least for now, lover."

"We have more time?"

"If you're nice."

"Meaning?"

"Meaning that I'm starving! You feel great but right now, so would a hamburger! Up, if you please!"

Not only did she insist. The delightful woman did so by working him over, all four of her limbs thrashing about. It was enough to cause their disengagement.

"But you only just finished eating."

"That was two hours ago. This is now!"

She rubbed her abdomen, feigning the worst sort of hunger and comical amazement at his lack of consideration. He'd give it his best.

"Look here. It's more than ten-thirty. There's no room service at this hour. I'll run down and get you something".

"No way! I'm coming too! Might even see something more interesting than a greasy old hamburger."

The electroencephalographer stayed in bed watching the beautiful young woman arise in her bared splendor, and head for the shower. When she returned, she moved gracefully through the room, methodically retracing steps formerly taken in haste as she recovered her discarded clothes, still strewn as she had dropped them in a line with the door. From every station of that retrieval, and before slipping into each garment, she turned, wafting him a kiss. What with his continuing desire, it was pretty stiff provocation. He managed to ease up on his singlemindedness, however, once recognizing the humor of the situation. In fact, he found himself grinning broadly, and though it was done rather sheepishly, he matched an airborne peck of his own to each of those dispatched in his direction. Life and love were holding sway. Everything in that room was eternal. There could be no descending feelings amidst all of that buoyancy.

Only when she was fully dressed and standing impatiently with hands fisted and braced against her hips, did he scramble from bed to attend his own needs. Also soon reconstituted, the electroencephalographer hugged her once more, but just to whisper a confidence in her elfin ear.

"I just remembered something."

"You're broke?"

"No. An interesting spot, and right down the street."

"You mean, like food interesting?"

"I'm sure. Up on top of a building. Called the Salvation Too."

"What in hell you up to now? You some kind of holy roller?"

"No way! It looked like a night club."

"You're on, brother! Get your buns together and let's move."

"You don't have a curfew, do you?"

"Christ, but you ask stupid questions! No I do not have a curfew! What I have is a grumbling stomach. You got it? Can we move on?"

Thirteen

Thus it came to pass that the electroencephalographer and his perfect female other self made their way downstairs and walked the half block distance to the nearby building where another elevator would raise them to the Salvation Too. Soon they were seated side by side on a couch from which they could look across a small table down into the park below. It was a mixed sort of crowd and also quite a young one as far as he could determine by looking into both the brightly lit and darker recesses of the room. Most of the clientele were in casual clothes. There were three couples in formal wear, but it was the waiters who were dressed in a really odd way. Each wore some kind of religious collar. While the woman began to munch peanuts at a quick pace, the electroencephalographer ordered a bottle of Haut Brion from one of the faux clergymen and requested the menu of an other. A four piece band positioned just beyond a small and empty dance floor was playing very softly, tempo variations on Amazing Grace.

She had snuggled up to whisper her appraisal of the establishment.

"Gross. This is gross."

"You're offended?"

"You kidding? Sorry, I forgot. You don't kid. You're only serious!"

"I had no idea. I've never been up here before this. Just saw it today from the street. Wild though, I agree, to have all these ministers, even a priest, hustling your food and drink."

Which is what was happening. And true to her promise of being able to improve upon a choice of ham burger, she ordered a rare filet mignon. The electroencephalographer went for a well done veal chop. In between peanuts, she continued.

"No. I'm not offended. It's anybody's world. They can do what they please just so long as they don't push me around, or try to lay something on me they know will bug me. I was only thinking there are lots of people out there down below who would be turned off by all of this, though I'm not one of them. Anyway, I sort of get this here message."

"What's that?"

"There are many ways to salvation. You know, for your soul."

"Depending upon the waiter you might just happen to draw, or the religion you might chance to be born into?"

"By George, I think you've got it!"

She crooked her finger inside his shirt collar, pulled him over and had his mouth to hers. The kiss was warm, wet, and not at all tidy. The electroencephalographer was quickly on the verge of going berserk because she was also pressing and pinching at his fly. When she started to lick his ear, he had to break away.

"Please, a little mercy! Or I'll pass out!"

They were interrupted by the wine service. As soon as the waiter had left she raised her glass in toast.

It was overstyled, dramatic. Then leaning across his shoulder she intruded her lips into his ear and began to murmur.

"Not on your life, not on your life, no mercy, not on your life ... "

"And why in hell not?"

"By George, you've got it again! You've managed to get it once more! Aren't you the smart one!"

This time her laughter was ribald to the point of causing heads to turn in almost every corner of the place.

"What's that supposed to mean?"

"You drunk again? Don't you remember? You asked why in hell? ... why in hell! Get it now?"

"No."

"We are all coping, darling. Coping with this place, which for each one of us is all there is, the one and only place. Coping with our hell. We drink, we dance, we pray, and we fuck one another. Get it? That's how we manage to get by, see our way through. Through our hell!"

"That's it? That's all there is?"

"Right. You go be the philosopher if you want. I say, if you do that, if you go for making more of it than it is, more than a hell, especially if you start living like it's some thing else, then you are just looking for big trouble and that's all you'll ever manage to find!"

Again, she raised her glass to toast him, downed the drink and looked away, staring up at the band. The electroencephalographer set himself to mechanically and numbly refilling their glasses. He needed to be in motion, any kind of motion. He had to overcome his inclination to just sit transfixed, shocked into immobility by what she'd just said. Why he could have been listening to himself, but himself in her voice!

"We're in hell? Earth is hell?"

"What earth, lover? Where's that?"

"And everything is only as we see it, feel it. It lacks other identity?"

"Right!"

"And don't sweat it or try to figure it out. Just deal with it? That's the way?"

"That's it, brother. It's our special rap."

"Maybe we should dance."

"Terrific. I'd love to dance with you."

"By the way, you never did say what you do."

"You never asked, you creep. I'm flight attendant Edna Morton of TWA."

It was a slow number and there were only two other couples on the floor. The electroencephalographer and the beautiful young woman held one another closely, swaying in place more than moving about to the music, some hard to make out vagary about "joy" and "finding a new friend" being sung into a microphone a bit vaingloriously by an all-smiling, light-skinned black fellow. The electroencephalographer sensed a commitment now to some new course.

Without any doubt, his encounter of the woman was not accidental. This had to be his other half he was holding fast to, right there on the dance floor. It stirred his recollection of the fabled Adam's rib. And was he going through what he had thought about before, what people called bonding? Well, he'd even have it one better than that. He'd fancy them melting down together, headed for a conjoined oblivion! There was also his amazement that, while this very morning, he was merely guessing at how best to provoke his fellow passengers aboard the train, only chancing to imagine the bunch of them all together on a roller coaster ride in hell, here, right here in New York, the same screw ball concept had already become an article of faith for this beauty of his, this Edna Morton, now being held securely in his arms! Of course, it was only allegorical. Earth was not hell! But there was, still, this uniquely common turn or was it twist of their minds? Had it drawn them to one another? Then came a queasy return of earlier sensations of the day, hinting at an obscure observing awareness directed upon him. And it was not just an exaggeration of the feeling, harbored by every self-conscious being, that to knowingly exist is to feel the presence of a somehow discerning universe.

"Hey, sweet girl. Looks like your steak is out."

"Great! Red meat! Now that's what I call my real thing!"

Taking him by the hand she just about jogged him back to their table.

Soon, with Edna dealing voraciously with her filet, and only pausing once in awhile to ecstatically drink to its excellence, the electroencephalographer fell to wondering why he had ordered for himself this additional evening meal. A strong appetite for food had never driven him. Eating was but an obligation, something needing to be gotten through by the clock, solely for the purpose of hanging on. In that respect at least, the woman and he were not at all alike. In fact, in many ways the electroencephalographer and she were very different. Her approach to living, it seemed, was lusty in every sense and her impatience with what she deemed the nonessentials, truly remarkable. One could not imagine her poking about in the dust bins of things remote or hung up on issues of no imminent consequence. This ideal other half of his was turning out to be some kind of practical minded hedonist. And now, even though his veal chop was barely picked over, she was chomping down a roll and studying the dessert menu.

"Perfect, lover! They have ice cream and strawberries!"

"You've got room?"

"You've got a problem?"

With her grabbing at his thigh to rebuke him, eyes narrowed down and mouth pouting displeasure over any such threatened denial, so taken was he by yet more of her cute ways, having a problem at this particular moment was not possible.

"Syrup?"

"Of course, silly. Let's make it chocolate."

"Chocolate it shall be!"

"I'm beginning to think a girl could really count on you!"

The steak was disposed of, the table cleared, and her dessert order placed, this time with an obsequious Baptist minister, oddly of Indian or Pakistani extraction. They leaned back to sip their wine and stare at the headlamps of traffic alternately flowing or moving erratically through the park below. The electroencephalographer had just about decided this was as good an opportunity as any to sneak in one of his newly devised states of mindlessness without her catching on to it, when a voice intruded.

"Having a good time?"

It was the vocalist apparently in a break between sets and moving about the room to greet and hobnob with his audience.

"Roger's the name. OK to join you?"

Assured of the privilege, he pulled up a chair and beer in hand, sat down smiling broadly.

"Why you've blue eyes, haven't you?" asked the woman.

"Passed down to me by one of my fast running Anglo Saxon ancestors" he quipped with a chesty chuckle. "There's things about you-all I've been noticing. Wanta hear them?"

The electroencephalographer, taking his cue from her assent also nodded his agreement. Might be interesting, perhaps, to hear what an uninformed bystander made of their pairing.

"No one moves like you two, not unless they've just met."

Seeming to need admission of that much, he was so favored.

"There, see, I knew it! Wanta know just how I knew?" Again, he got the green light.

"My life, my entire trip is music, rhythm, how things move through time and in time. Dig?"

So far it could hardly seem anything other than plausible.

"That's what it's all about. Everything is just what happens because of time. Without time, nothing is possible, nothing is cool. And when people start travelling through time together, they've got their own special rhythm. That is, until maybe they start having second thoughts, or kind of get too used to one another, or let themselves be influenced by what someone else might say about them hangin' together. Then that's it, that's the end of it, the end of their perfect little rhythm, which is what you two have right now. Get it? There isn't anything but time, no me, no you, all we are is so many frequencies in time. There's frequency of light, and of sound, and of hitting on one another, and of getting into things together, and of getting it on together, and of me and of all of us. Now you two, right now, are like atoms that have crashed into one another and are set to vibrating like crazy, like just crazy, like wow! Anyone can see it. You've got it, but only together, because you are really together, like what they call a nova!"

Roger fell back in his chair, obviously pleased with the surety of his powers of both observation and theoretical disputation. The young woman was on him quickly. She snapped."Roger, you're full of it. Take my advice brother and just stick with the music. I don't know what anything is really all about. But you, you know even less than me! You gain' back on tonight?"

"Sure. In just three minutes."

"How about something with a little beat next set, and for Christ sake, not so damned slow! Maybe if you had your mind on what you're supposed to be doing up there, and weren't such a fucking snoop, we'd all of us be having a better time! And it seems to me you goof off too much. You're leaning on your side men, not tending to business. Other than that you could be the greatest! Love your voice! Like the way you wiggle your butt! Just forget the god damned philosophy. No point in it. Pisses everybody off! Me in particular!"

With Roger in fast retreat, she turned to the electro-encephalographer.

"Where are my strawberries, lover?"

He, quick to respond and pretending fear for the con sequences should her newly staged militancy be directed next toward him, summoned a clergyman and demanded fast and better service or they'd quit the place. Those theatrics gaining her an immediate and quite robust serving of what she wanted, he sat back having been impressed once again by the beautiful woman's amazing directness. Roger, rejoined with his band and singing away, was apparently taking her advice to heart. Edna was now dealing with the challenge of spooning dessert to mouth with one hand the while finger-tapping an appropriate tempo upon the electroencephalographer's outstretched palm with the other. Then, having downed one last strawberry, she slipped her arm around him and set herself to scratching at a loin already in a steady state of yearning.

"Where you based?" came his quivering question out of a mouth made dry once more by all of this excitement.

"Right here, my home town, the big apple."

"Ever get to Washington?"

"Once and awhile. You inviting me?"

"Absolutely! When's your next flight?"

"Tomorrow night. Paris. Want to come?"

"Don't I wish! No such luck."

"Well then let's get up. We'll dance some more, maybe fly a little right here!"

It was dancing now of a different sort, requiring skills not of the electroencephalographer's own era. He was forced to keep in a centered position on the floor, holding to the beat with impromptu but conservative movements of his own design, the while she executed all sorts of high stepping and hip swinging outrage. From her smile he would have thought she was thoroughly enjoying herself. It was certainly a stupendous sight, this dynamo of female allurement, wriggling and squirming all over the place, and it was so publicly and flatteringly directed toward him that he was exulting in it. It came, therefore, as a surprise when all of a sudden she stopped and went back quickly to their table.

Her demand, characteristically, was simply stated. "Let's get the hell out of here!"

"Something wrong?"

"It's not for us. We'll go somewhere else."

"OK. Whatever you want."

"No, it's got to be a place you know and that *you* like."

"To tell the absolute truth, before I met you this evening, I was kind of escorted out of what up until then was my hands down favorite place, the Saint Regis. You know the King Cole Bar?"

"Why'd they kick you out?"

"Over drinks. Somebody lost count."

"You mean like too many for drinking and driving?"

"Amazing! That's exactly how one guy put it! But not really. More like I thought someone stole my martini. Then I became sort of ugly, and you might say in more ways than one, got carried away and then out of the place."

"Anybody ever suggest you could use help, I mean like the professional kind?"

"No, but I like the idea. How about me making my mind a blank and having you analyze me?"

"Forget it! And I don't want some damned bar! Even if it's your favorite."

"Well, there's also the Regis Roof. I suppose we might be able to slip through the lobby and upstairs before that house dick spots me again. As I remember, it's a beautiful place. Wonderful orchestra. Went there once almost twenty years ago with a girl who didn't care for me too much. In fact, the very next week she ran off to Chicago and got married."

"Spare me the gory details. If you like it, then that's our ticket. We're on our way!"

The electroencephalographer paid the tab, shrugged off a blessing tendered back at him along with his credit card, and descended to street level still holding tightly to his deliciously compliant other half. It was so straightforward and natural by now to walk with her like that, that he began dreading the prospect of walking again, after this night, on his solitary own. But such apprehension only inclined him to indulge his pleasure in joined movement all the more, as if needing now to stock up on enough of it to carry him through tough times ahead. That's how they hastened along together over the five block distance back to the Saint Regis Hotel. The same house detective was, in fact, sitting in the lobby; however, either he failed to recognize the electroencephalographer in the woman's company, or he decided to let him pass unmolested, since he had accepted his earlier eviction so agreeably.

An elevator raced them aloft to the Roof, a magnificently enclosed space of french doors, pink damasked walls, flashing crystal chandeliers, deep piled floor coverings, and a slippery smooth dance floor. The musicians, in black tie, were playing "Just in Time," and rather jauntily so. His companion was overwhelmed.

"Wow! And you took me to that creepy place?"

"How was I to know? I'd never been there before!"

The captain took their coats, and quickly ushered them to the only remaining table. One look at this woman and there was none of the usual nonsense about needing reservations. She did not turn heads. She disintegrated them!

"Could I have one more dessert?"

"And?"

"Not wine. Maybe a cognac."

"What kind of dessert? Need the menu?"

"No. I know just what I want and they can make it without any trouble at all."

The electroencephalographer summoned a waiter, then listened disbelievingly to her residual needs.

"Just bring me a plate of vanilla ice cream with lots of pineapple slices and ... "

"Of course, miss."

"Hey, hold your horses, buddy. I'm not quite through. You have to pour a little anisette over it. And in case it's not just right, I want a jigger of anisette on the side. It's called a pineapple something or other. I forget exactly what, but it's dynamite!"

The electroencephalographer could not get enough of this woman or her ways. He loved her. He loved her enough to just about cry over it. Except that he couldn't. He'd not be declaring anything with tears. He'd have to settle for mere words.

"I'm in love with you. There's no doubt about it."

"My god, are we going to have to put up with that? Look, we're just gonna concentrate on having a good time. Finally you've brought me to a real nice joint. So let's have us a ball. It is kind of like a ballroom, don't you think?"

"Hear what they're playing?"

"Nice, but I don't know it."

"It's Long Before I Knew You, an old number from Bells Are Ringing. Want the lyrics?"

"Sure."

The electroencephalographer took her hand and explained how by the song it was possible to know that one would assuredly meet, someday, the "one" who would walk and talk as she did.

She leaned across the table and kissed him softly on the cheek.

"Nice try, lover. But that's only a different spin on all that old Maurice Chevalier crap. You know, the nonsense about some girl maybe passing you by without you ever getting to know it's that certain one, the one of your dreams, your ideal. At least this little ditty they're playing n ow, gets them together and doesn't have us needing to put up with some damned cry baby."How could she know his favorite Chevalier number but only to regard it so differently? What end to this evolving mystery?

"Not very sentimental, are you?"

"Well, not in a damn fool way."

"You think crying is wrong?"

"You gonna start bawling?"

"I never do. I can't cry."

"Hot dog! I'm spared that! Now look here!" She elbowed him in the side. "You plan on dancing anymore tonight or do we just sit here and soul search or talk about some pretty dumb lyrics?"

The electroencephalographer led her on to this other
dance floor. Although it was crowded he could do much
better here than at the Salvation Too. The orchestra was
playing well and in a way that found him better able to
respond. He liked the brightly polished ambience of the
room and the cheerful, even-mannered sportings of the
well groomed clientele. And it was such bliss to be seen
in the company of this absolute jewel. Soon he was marvelling at himself for the way he could swirl and guide her,
almost miraculously finding spaces between other couples
exactly on the moment they materialized, as if those dancing corridors were there by his command. He thought it
quite magical. Never much of a dancer, he was certain
his performance was an accomplishment drawing entirely
upon her influence. To dance with anyone else could be no
more than so much obligatory and convivial heavy-footed
holding to a beat. Edna had surmised as much.

"Hey, why didn't you tell me? You're quite the dancer,
aren't you? So light on your feet! Lead on, lover!"

They danced right through to the end of the set, then
stood breathing fast and perspiring a little, while applaud-
ing along with the others. As soon as they were re-seated,
the waiter brought her dessert and two glasses of cognac.
She was prepared now to be generous to the electroencephalographer.

"Want some?"

"Not really. Looks straightforward enough."

"C'mon, have a taste!"

"Very interesting. Kind of a licorice flavor."

"That's the anisette. That guy I was with. He introduced me to it."

"You didn't say what he did."

"Christ, you do have a peculiar way of asking questions, don't you? As if everybody is somehow holding out on you! Now ask it properly!"

"What's he do? God damn it!"

"I suppose that could pass. He's a photographer. It all started when I modelled for him. You saw when it ended. Very civilized."

"Anyone else?"

"There's always someone else. That's if you're really alive, there is. I mean, you know, going and coming, about every year or two. But just one at a time. I'm not one of those very modern girls, the ones you see hopping around from stud to stud, like they're on a carousel."

"And me?"

"You? I met you like ten minutes ago and you ask a silly fool question like that? Besides, you talk too much. And your mind wanders all over the place! Just imagine, as good as you are at it, how much better still you'd be as a dancer, and also at what you could accomplish in the play pen, if only you'd concentrate, put your mind to it, to just a few things. It gives me goose bumps just thinking about it! Hell, you'd sweep every damned girl right off her feet and into the sack! Wouldn't that be so much better than all of this dumb talk, talk, talk?"

Heads were turning again at the sound of her hearty follow-up laughter. She moved to force him along and into her jubilance by chucking him under the chin and pinching mercilessly at his ribs. The result was that the electroencephalographer was finding himself increasingly aware of how unfamiliar was this new territory. To be tossed about by so much mirth and high-spirited turbulence was not easy to deal with. It was hard also to reconcile his newly-come-by euphoria with the long-entrenched oppressive nature of his usual concerns. And he knew full well they were only waiting for another go at him. But those glum premonitions could be staved off, at least for the time being, by his resolve to dance and to drink his way against them. That, the beautiful woman and he managed to do quite well until the room closed down at two a.m. By then, he had become so good at his facile movements on the dance floor he even drew kindhearted praise from the orchestra leader. But now it was over and he beckoned again for the tab.

"The bill please, waiter."

"Thank god! You've just about wiped me out. Now tell me your name again? Wasn't it Adlai?"

"Adam, Adam Turner."

"Well thank you Adam Turner for what was a lovely time."

"You leaving me now?"

"You lost your mind completely?"

When they were back down on the street and standing under the marquee, the electroencephalographer hauled the woman to him by her coat collar and mumbled in her ear.

"What smells so inviting? Is it you? Is it the fur? The perfume?"

"Nice of you to say so, but actually I could use an other shower! C'mon, let's get on back to your place."

Unaccountably, the electroencephalographer threw his arm skyward and called out.

"Taxi!"

"Now you're some kind of comedian? The Park Lane is only up the street. Or are you so stoned you don't even know where in hell you are?"

"Taxi!" he screamed again.

The doorman (not the same fellow who had brushed him aside so adeptly earlier in the day), with a five dollar tip from the electroencephalographer freshly in hand, swept them grandly into a cab which had screeched to a stop on being summoned by his whistle. As the door slammed shut, the electroencephalographer gave directions to the driver.

"The Park Lane!"

"You kiddin', mister?" She interceded.

"No driver, he's not. He's just a bit cuckoo. If we humor him, he'll probably get over it."

"Lady, the Park Lane is only a coupla blocks! God damn it! Walk it! My wife I gotta humor. Nuts, I kick in the ass!"

The electroencephalographer was prepared to be insistent. "Look here, fella. You know full well you can't just toss us out. I'm within my rights. Once that door closed on us, you took the fare for wherever and whatever!"

"Mister, I'm waitin' more than an hour for a good one, like LaGuardia or somethin' downtown. Now you've got me losin' my place in the lineup fer absolutely nothin'. C'mon, be a nice guy and get the hell outa here!"

"OK, let's have LaGuardia and then the Park Lane.

You want a nice guy, I'll show you a real one!" The woman got in her own lick.

"Now stop it! Just stop it! Behave yourself! Let's get out and right now. I don't have time for this. We're not going on any round trip to LaGuardia! Be a nice boy, lover, or I'm splittin'!"

"Tell you what, driver. Head for the Park Lane before that light turns red, and you've got yourself the LaGuardia tab but only the flat rate mind you, and no tolls!"

"You're on!"

The woman yelled out to anyone inclined to listen, what could, at the electroencephalographer's risk, be her final view of things.

"I knew it, I knew it! He has really lost his mind! Completely lost his everlovin' mind!"

The cabbie tore away from the curb, even making the light well before the amber, and jerked to a stop at the Park Lane in a flat forty seconds. The electroencephalographer had certified the result by craning his neck and making appropriate verification from what he could see of the traffic light through the cab's rear window. Now every one was celebrating and in a much better mood.

"Mister, I gotta hand it to you. You're an all right dude!"

"No, I'm handing it to you. Thirty-five do it?"

"Perfect. And it sure beats standin' in line or guzzlin' gas all the way out to LaGuardia. Have a good one!"

The cab was gone and she was standing in front of the hotel regarding him curiously.

"You mind letting me in on what that was all about?"

"I'm crazy for you and didn't want you to walk it. It's cold. That's all."

"I'm just a glorified air-borne waitress, up on my poor tired feet all day, all night, at seven thousand feet and five hundred miles an hour, and you, Adam Turner, you don't want me having to walk?"

"What you do on your time is your business. When you're with me, I'd like to make a difference."

Already, there had been kisses, lots of kisses. The one she gave him now was of a different vintage. It tasted serious. It would be the same with the one that followed. What else to consider them, he thought, but as having meaning? Eyeing him sternly, she reached up and took him by the ear, not letting go until she had him on the elevator. Then this new kind of kissing was resumed until the elevator opened to their floor. Each subsequent move, each step toward his room, the unlocking of the door, their entering, undressing, falling into bed, were all occasions for these new kinds of kisses. Until finally they seemed to reach a mutual understanding that so much gravity was, in its own odd way, too offbeat, too hilarious to bear with, and so when finally they did come together again, it was with a giggle.

Fourteen

It was a first, the novel feeling he'd not slept alone. Yet on awakening, alone was how he found himself in that bed, and in that room. He could remember, gratifyingly, the unparalleled vigor she had aroused. He could also recall being finally expended and succumbing to sleep still joined to her. Before dropping off there had been some wondering about just why it was that men feared to die during intercourse, even in circumstances that did not involve an illicit relationship. But last night he had not given a hoot. In fact, of all possible ways to die, doing so in her arms, and during such release, was all he might want for himself. And to be with her seemed now the only real way to not feel alone.

He panicked, therefore, at finding himself in this barrenly empty hotel room. He was also somewhat the worse for the effects of too much alcohol. Head throbbing, mouth dry, he got to his feet, only to find he was also nauseated and unsteady. The physical problems were no rival, how ever, for his anxiety not to have found her still there beside him. Obviously, she had dressed and slipped away. He might just as well be dead.

How was he to find her again? He hadn't even a phone number! Perhaps through TWA. That and a name were all he had. But suppose it was all fabrication. Suppose there was no Edna Morton in fact working for TWA, and she was gone, disappeared forever? Christ, the thought of it was unendurable! He began to perspire profusely, felt the need to douse with cold water, and headed for the bathroom.

When he looked up from the sink in that small room, a place provided mere mortals to cleanse and to relieve themselves, it became suddenly the most splendid spot in all the universe! She was there! Well, not really she herself, but rather a message from her. Scrawled on the mirror in smears of fleshy pink lipstick was his suddenly revived possibility of somehow breaking out and also the immediate remedy for his morning despair. Unsteady or not, he'd be dancing again, and maybe even right then and there! "Gone for my uniform. Back by ten. Order me pan cakes and sausages and more strawberries. Screw the Metroliner! You're going to the airport with me!"

She'd worked it all out! There'd be a full day together. Well then, it had better be a level headed one for sorting things out and for planning how to keep this match of theirs on track! But by the time he'd finished shaving, and showering raucously to his own rendition of Just in Time, I Found You Just in Time!, he was confounded at how much he wanted her again. How could he, at his age, be so quickly rejuvenated into what seemed a steady state of arousal? And though that might be an optimal condition for their further enjoyment of one another during the rest of this day, it hardly promised to facilitate the kind of deliberation he was thinking very much in order.

He had to towel up because someone was pounding at the door. Cracking it open, he had the only sight he wanted.

"Got my breakfast?"

"First my morning kiss. Then I order it."

"Okay, but just a quickie, I'm starving! There, that should do until you call it in. Meanwhile, I'll just get comfortable again. Got a robe for me?"

"There's a Hers in the bathroom."

"Imagine! Never noticed any thing of that sort around here last night, what with all the monkey business going on."

"You been seeing monkeys?"

"Just the one big baboon, lover. Be right back."

The electroencephalographer found the repartee delightful but, all the same, he was thinking of other things. Mainly, he was struck by how different she looked in day light, particularly how young and vulnerable she seemed. That impression was exaggerated by her trim white blouse and blue uniform. He was reminded of adolescent girl scouts and those teenage girl ushers there used to be years ago in the larger movie houses. Amazing how she could make him think like that and yet be more fundamentally known to him as a strong willed woman, inordinately insistent about how she'd have her pleasures. He called down the breakfast order. The kitchen was prompt in responding and soon there was loud knocking to announce its arrival as well as countering vibrations from the bathroom.

"You gonna let the man in with my vittles or do I have to come on out the way I am and flip a few people?" He, made now the arch joker by gift of her kind second coming, called back through the bathroom door. "You're nuts if you think that would bother anyone!

But you can come on out. The guy's gone. Everything is all here and it's hot. Let's just not have a damned stampede!" Robed in white terry cloth, she dashed to the table, eyes agleam with anticipation.

"Does that ever look good! Quick, put some of it back in the warmer! Let's not have anything getting cold!"

A glance was all he'd had from her. The focus was entirely on the food.

"Hello there! Remember me?"

"Later, lover. I'm tending to important business! What do the football people call it? Major jumbo?"

"Whatever."

He had never seen pancakes get swamped by so much maple syrup. That is, the ones she did not thoroughly jelly over. She'd sample one kind, then the other, and also take eye rolling bites out of sausages and croissants. Once having eliminated this abundance, she set herself to attacking what had been put aside in the warmer.

"Don't see how you can settle for a mere English muffin, lover."

"We older ones tend to put on weight."

"Never gonna happen to me!"

"Just wait. See if it doesn't."

"Waiting is not my way! I'm too big on instant gratification!"

"Thank the good something or other for that!"

Once there was nothing left of either the pancakes or

the rest of her main course and even the serving dishes had been dealt a scrupulous regoing over, this Edna Morton of his fell back into bed nibbling on strawberries and demanding conversation.

"Well all right, talk to me."

"Your name really Edna Morton?"

"Last I knew it was. Why? Shouldn't it be?"

"I was just scared when I found you were gone. I thought, what if it was for good without your even having left me a genuine clue?"

"You're not a very good judge of character."

"No way to practice and get better at it. I kind of keep to myself, you know. Just roll with the punches, try to decipher the everyday nitty-gritty. Never been much for people and their intrigues. Nor had much time for any thing but the essences, the roots of things."

"Christ, here we go again! Giddyap horsie, I'm leaving!"

"It was you who wanted to talk."

"Sure, but let's keep it light."

"How in hell can I do that, the way I feel about you?"

"Look, let's make a deal. If in thirty years you're in the same mood you think you're in right now, then that'll be plenty time and we can get down to brass tacks."

She chortled and grabbed for his ribs. He was immune to the maneuver, being not at all ticklish. He was far from immune, however, to her other playfully endearing ways and didn't require, in fact, any arousal other than what was already his by the privilege of having read on the bath room mirror her promise to return. After a few moments of light-hearted wrestling their robes were tossed aside and the clowning gave way to the kind of repositioning he could be absolutely satisfied with, just about forever.

Morning passed into afternoon. Their ardor was interrupted only briefly by a twenty minute nap and quick lunch, consisting of a Reuben sandwich and apple pie for her, turkey on rye for him. At four PM it was getting time to depart. The electroencephalographer sensed the precipitous downturn of his spirits even before her announcement of it.

"We have to go. I'll shower first."

It was her opening move toward the impending severance.

"I'd rather not feel alone until I have to. Let's shower together."

It was not to be just a shower. With her or not with her, it was an immersion in dread even though she laughed and high jinxed her way through it in her unique way. He couldn't manage even a half-hearted response. To be cut off from this body which had rippled so delightfully, under and around him, was scarcely bearable. But also to be exiled from her impish spirit and to face falling back into his obdurately obsessive and morose ways might easily not be tolerable at all.

"I don't like the way you're looking at me, lover! The world is not coming to an end just yet. C'mon, we're gonna get dressed."

When they each had their clothes back on and had gathered up their belongings, she seated herself at a small desk, took paper in hand, and scribbled: "EDNA MORTON your New York girl," along with a Second Avenue address and phone number.

"If I'm not there, my roommate's name is Gwen."

"Cell phone?"

"Too burdensome."

Give me your parents' number then."

"No way."

"Why not?"

"My mother might take a shine to you."

Her uniform was getting to him. Somehow he was beginning to think it sexier than last night's black dress. He didn't dare speculate too much on how every guy who looked, might also turn on to the sight of her in it.

"Ready?"

"No!"

"C'mon, I'll lose my job!"

"One more kiss?"

"No way! We'll never get out of here! But I promise you this. You'll have a big one in the taxi, one that will last all the way out to Kennedy. We won't even come up for air!"

She was good to her word. That was precisely how they traveled. The electroencephalographer saw nothing of their passage to the airport. There were only her green eyes, soft brown hair, those fabulous ankles, the warm moist thrustings of her tongue, and the insistent pressure of her lips. When the taxi pulled up at TWA terminal she broke away and exited. He jumped out, grabbing her once again.

"When?"

"The ball's in your court, lover."

A peck on his cheek, a turn to wave, and she was gone.

His knees were letting go. His throat was in cruel contraction. Something unpleasant was taking place in the upper abdomen. The electroencephalographer wanted to run after her, but could not allow himself to seem that foolish, that immature. He retreated back into the taxi.

"Pan Am, driver, and Hell, or aren't we already there?"

"What you say, man?"

"Forget it. Let's just go to Pan Am."

Fifteen

The next Pan Am flight for Washington would be at 10:10. It was only six. The electroencephalographer had the alternative of cabbing back to LaGuardia and making the seven o'clock shuttle. He supposed he could, but why bother? What was the point? What difference where, if not with her? And at Kennedy he could at least fancy her nearby. No, he'd not go to LaGuardia. He'd settle for a close by sense of the woman Edna until Paris bound TWA 745 showed on the board as having departed.

He bought his ticket and took a seat in the departure lounge. Now he was aware of certain residual hangover symptoms, most of which had so miraculously dissipated with discovery of her morning promise to get back to him at the Park Lane. They were returned in the form of mild headache and a sense of being drained. Could he work a similar relief just by thinking of the prospects for their eventual reunion, picking willy nilly any old date and time? He tried, and the thought of it seemed to assuage his physical distress, but only just a bit.

Imaginings these, and she now no more than that. Edna had become only what could be recalled or imagined. Except for the actual moments of a happening, did anything really ever count for more? In the end, what difference was there even between an imagined event and one that had, in fact, occurred? Was not universal oblivion certain to be unsparing of both? There was a difference, perhaps, and it was meager. It was only that the fancied, the hallucinated, was flawed for lacking reasonable hope of recurrence. But even there the difference might be slim. Dreams did have their way of repeating, and the crazies indulged their fantasies over and over again. Christ, he considered, if a thing was not to be taken immediately, grabbed for by its substance, squeezed for by its flesh, then it counted for nothing! So what genuine distinction now between Edna as a real life, hot blooded siren and some torturing, dream-based temptress of a drunk who'd been tossed, and quite rightly so, out of the King Cole Bar? A guy who feeling miserable, just toppled into bed to awaken at four pm the next day and had to hurry home, his mind a mix of grief and fantasy.

Maybe if he had a drink he would feel better, manage somehow to right this quandary, and like they say, fight fire with fire. Anything to get a hold on himself. He re called also something about having the hair of what one has been bitten by. The electroencephalographer slid into a seat at the bar adjoining the Pan Am departure lounge and ordered a vodka tonic.

It was his habit to take vodka in former days when he drank and didn't want people to be aware of it. He had never had any real hankering for vodka. How could any one like what had no significant taste? But there were connoisseurs in the world for everything, it seemed, even for things that had no taste. In any event, vodka placed little odor on the breath, so he could get away with it if he took some now. The electroencephalographer ordered what he wanted from a pretty bartender.

Well yes, he realized she was pretty. Like now he also realized there were planes to be seen out the window taxiing between the gates and runways, taking off, landing, having a busy old time of it. But only one person was pretty in a way that had significance. That was Edna, out there somewhere, getting herself ready to take off, perhaps moving up and down the aisle in that unsettling little blue uniform and showing off her ankles, probably driving other men nuts. That was what pretty was about! It wasn't the bar girl's kind of pretty. He supposed that once most guys were sexually aroused, as he was still, they would target any attractive woman within their sights. Kind of like getting fixated, locked in by their hormones, their drive centers. He remembered one writer going so far as to say that when he chanced to love a particular woman, he found he loved all women. That had seemed a very peculiar bit of thinking to the electroencephalographer's mind. Giving the same thought some further room to roam, to kind of wander through the ranks of all kinds of women, the idea of that was actually revolting to him! So this bar girl was only pretty in an abstract way. That would be particularly so because in the past, when lovelorn in an unrequited fashion, the electroencephalographer had never been able to find solace in the company of other women as surrogates for someone else. They had only made him think, or yearn, after his real love, and were diminished by any attempt at comparison with her. Such had been the painful circumstance of several involvements. Relief came only by finally riding out his feelings, until, like most others, they would let up with time. But when he was victim to them, those feelings never seemed likely either to ease or to end. So now, about all he had to see him through his heartache was the theory it would subside eventually, as all things did. Yes, the bar girl could be cute. She could be pretty as all hell! For all he cared, she could even be stark naked! But she was only for handing him a drink. There could be no meaning in it for him when she smiled so sweetly on his ordering of the second.

Picking up a phone to call his house in Washington, he matter-of-factly projected a late hour of arrival. His wife seemed cheerful and asked after his friend Jean. It was troubling to realize Jean had just about slipped from his sphere of concerns. He would need to call her. After quickly summarizing for his wife the visit with his ailing friend, he telephoned Jean as well. Nothing much different going on there. She was leaving imminently for her special radiation treatment in California, and still so under protest from her New York doctors. He wished her well and hung up quickly, before, in her god-awful condition, she might again concern herself over him and his much more viable welfare. He had had quite enough angst by now without also being made to feel again that damned guilt and sensitivity for the selfish and unconventional ways in which he went about his own life-grubbing business.

An older fellow, also at the bar, moved closer to get his ear.

"Never do know when you're getting home these days, do you?"

The electroencephalographer always ignored such overtures, and simply sat staring into empty space, hoping the other would give up on him. He certainly did not want, at that moment, to be bothered by some old duffer needing company. Why couldn't people be satisfied with the fellowship of their own thoughts, or find other amusements? Why did they have to make nuisances of them selves? All he wanted to do now was think about Edna, out there somewhere in her blue uniform.

"I say, what with all the delays, you never do know when you're going to get back home, do you?"

Still the man got no answer, just barely a look from the electroencephalographer.

"You hard of hearing? Speak English?"

"I hear and I speak quite well."

"Then why didn't you answer me?"

"I don't have anything to say about it. Nor do I care much about the question you're raising with me."

"Hell! Everybody's got some kind of opinion on that!"

"Then everybody does minus one, this one, me! Can you manage that kind of arithmetic?"

"You're a real ball buster! You know that?"

"Wrong again. I'm nothing. You're nothing. So where we go and when we get there is of absolutely no consequence."

"Yeah? Well you try telling that to the little woman!"

"I don't have a little woman. My woman is big, big in

every way that matters. And right now at this very moment she is probably pouring herself a drink, and not particularly caring about when I may or may not get home."

"You through telling me off?"

"Never did anything of the kind. Take the time to think it over and you'll see I'm right."

The older man moved away shaking his head. The electroencephalographer remained in his seat at the bar, swivelling his drink, squeezing segments of lime into it, and staring back at his own image reflected off the window glass, now completely darkened over, the sun having set. That is one hell of a sorry looking slob, he thought, what for missing his dynamite gal! Wouldn't it be some thing, though, if the reflected one would just wise up, run like hell, and board that TWA 745 for Paris! Christ, the look there'd be on her face! He'd kiss her hand every time she brought him food or drink! He'd stand at her station and sweet talk her all the way across! And then, when they landed in Paris, off he'd go with her to the Ritz Hotel to cavort and to make love right through an other fantastic night! What could be more reasonable than that? What was the damned fool waiting for? He stared at the image of himself, somehow half expecting it to stir independently of him and to get on with it. What more was needed? What possible constraints were operating, now that this proposed scenario was so neatly in place and requiring only of the acting out? Was his self, as reflected, just one other of those ineffectual, interminably posturing, preening, and self-glorifying human clowns so adept at empty role playing to ends of no conceivably important consequence, but impotent for real and purposeful action? The image glared back at him and did not budge. He examined his watch. Seven fifteen and still ample time to catch up with her! If he would only get himself going he might not even have to run for it. He could just about stroll over to TWA. As he always kept his passport with him, at the ready for either travel or identification purposes, there would not even be that impediment. But the image stayed frozen in place with drink in hand, obscured in shadows, empty eyed, for lorn, obviously not impelled to do anything. It had the air of powerless acceptance and resignation.

These two finally did get around to doing something about their beloved Edna. Together, man and image searched an inside coat pocket to finger the only link remaining with the young woman of the blue uniform existing somewhere out beyond the window glass. But the pocket was empty! The slip of paper upon which she had inscribed, for his reassurance, what mattered most to him, was not there. Alarmed at not finding it, he rushed his hands through all his other pockets, then his bag, even the envelope holding his plane ticket. Her note had disappeared! Where could it have gotten to? Did it drop from his pocket when he was back in the cab, while they were embracing?

Damnation! He'd really need his keen memory to bail him out of this one! For sure, he'd looked intently enough at the note when she had handed it over to have confidence for remembering its substance this short a time afterward. Quickly, on the back of his boarding pass, he hastened to jot down her phone number, the address, and the room-mate's name as he recalled them. It all came so quickly and assuredly to mind he had little reason to doubt his accuracy. The name Edna Morton, of course, was not ever possible to be forgotten.

He had finished his vodka tonic. No need for any more drinking. He probably had everything back in hand. Perhaps so, but even a little reason to harbor doubt can be overwhelming if one is the electroencephalographer. And so a new question crossed his mind. It had actually been shaping itself steadily after having come into being the moment he saw her phone number again as it trailed behind the tip of his ballpoint pen moving to effect its recovery. The intruding thought was that both the telephone number and the person must be verified. But why? Did not Edna's uniform establish her, make her the genuine article? Yes, but he had to be dead sure his memory had not failed him and because he could not bear any possible uncertainty for any part of this colossal matter! He had to be reassured absolutely! If his recall of it was not as certain as he thought, or if (how killing the idea!) it was not the truth when she penned it, then he must know it and be desolate at once! He had to begin dealing with that calamity. Could he not await such remote eventuality until later and then track her down by her job, by the blue uniform? No! It all had to be cleared up and to be started on right then and there!

He reached for the phone at the end of the bar and dialed the number. The line was busy. What in hell did that mean? It meant that at least he had a working number. But whose number? He was not the kind of fellow to take it for the obvious, for the likelihood her roommate, the person Gwen, was probably using the phone and tying up the line.

Just how long now was this anxiety going to have its hold? He dialed the number again. Still busy. No way for him to reason away this sudden turmoil! Could the phone be off the hook? He got the operator. She assured him that was not the case. The line was truly engaged. The operator also refused to cut in. That would require some kind of emergency. To verify her name was Gwen or that her roommate's name was Edna, could not be considered one. He picked up a copy of the Manhattan telephone directory. No Edna Morton. Not even an E. Morton. So what? Probably, like every third or fourth person these days, she had an unlisted number. Yes, but what might be the real reason she had refused to give him her parents' phone number? He dialed once more. Still busy. What was happening to him?'Something mean was gripping him, and it had him feeling badly in so many different ways. He was anxious, alone, incomplete, separated, lost, bereft, helpless. He,needed to make some kind of contact again, any kind, no matter how indirect, no matter how implausible, with his darling Edna. Anything to stop this devilish hounding!

He called TWA. They had a rigidly held to policy. They could not give out or even verify the names of flight personnel. They certainly would not comment whether or not an Edna Morton was heading for Paris. It was getting worse, this peculiar thing in him which had him. If only he had seen some kind of pin with her name on it! Why hadn't he looked more closely or gone through her purse for an ID? All he had was a stupid phone number, and an address that might or might not be right! And if in fact there was a Gwen, and if that was their number, it was staying busy. Staying busy on purpose, to frustrate him. And so it did, for the innumerable times he dialed it. The electroencephalographer alternately labored, without luck, at dialing that number and pacing up and down the corridor near his departure gate. Hours later, when he made his flight to Washington he had still not succeeded. He boarded, a grieving failure.

On the trip back home there prevailed this fearful dilemma, a new one to which he was not accustomed, and as disturbing as his old fancied premonitions of imminent death. Was this what came of uninhibited attachment, of automatic commitment in love? Then Christ! Love and death, like reality and imaginings, what difference was there between them, either? They were much the same too, weren't they? Love and death were all that truly mattered and yet they were identical as well, because nothing, absolutely nothing at all, could be done to cure the agony of knowing them!

When the electroencephalographer deplaned at National Airport he went for the phone again and dialed the New York number. Busy! He took a taxi. Finally from his home, at last a ring signal. But no one picked up on it. With drowsiness he seemed to hear an interminable ringing noise. He fell asleep to that sound, but in time it became inflected, musical once more. The intonation of that ancient signal of sorts? But no answer for him in any of it, from anyone or anywhere.

Awakening the next day, still no response at the New York number. Was the roommate Gwen, herself now out bound to some distant place? And where in hell was Edna, if in fact she was really Edna? All needed to be dealt with, but he had to get back to the lab.

His technician was anxious.

Sixteen

"Doctor Cohen has been looking for you since Friday. He just missed you around noon and you didn't come back after lunch!"

"I had important personal business. What's he want?"

"Needs your opinion on a tracing."

"What's the rush?"

"It's a psychiatry patient over on Nine South. I ran her EEG after you left. The name's Mary O'Neil and they've got her on something experimental. Cohen looked at it himself and we both think it's kind of unusual. The waves are mostly frontal, but you're the expert, not us. Here comes Cohen again now. He's real excited about it."

Doctor Cohen was one of the young residents on psychiatry. A few months earlier, during a neurology elective,

he had chosen to spend time with the electroencephalographer out of curiosity regarding EEG. It was not a
required part of his training. He was simply fascinated by
brain waves and seemed to labor under the same naive
notions once belonging to the electroencephalographer in
his own early years that brain waves might be correlated
with mental activities. Back on psychiatry again, Cohen
was ordering EEGs like mad on every disturbed patient
assigned to him. The electroencephalographer, in fact, had
been intending to request a little more forbearance on his
part. Cohen was threatening to overload the schedule and
to interfere with getting the really important cases done.
Now, he rushed upon the electroencephalographer, who
had been taking his morning coffee and was staring at a
travel poster stuck to the wall near one of his machines. It
was of the Champs Elysee and maybe Edna as well. The
electroencephalographer was seeking after her blue uniform
amidst the strolling crowds.

"Doctor Turner, have you seen it, the tracing?"

"Not yet. What's the story?"

"It's a case of very severe depression in a woman who
has hardly talked to anybody in two weeks. We just started
her on HR335."

"Am I supposed to know what that is?"

"One of six new phenothiazine derivatives we're testing.
It's got some kind of tricky side chain variation. I'm no
biochemist and neither is the chief. He just said to put her
on it because nothing else has worked. Even electroshock
turned out to be a zero. This lady is really some thing! If
one of the experimental drugs doesn't help, the chief might
even recommend psychosurgery."

"That's all we need! Last time somebody in your crazy

department got that bright idea and ordered a prefrontal lobotomy, we had pickets out front for two months. They were even busloadin' 'em in! Could hardly get our own selves inside the place what for all the screaming human rights groups blocking everything off!"

"Really? Guess I wasn't around then."

"No, you were just a baby."

"So you going to read it? I think the tracing is one kind of weird EEG, myself."

"Cohen, is that the extent of what you learned in this laboratory? Did we waste our time on you entirely? An EEG has waves that are slow, or fast, or in between. They can be of high, or low, or medium voltage. Or if you like, you can measure these things and give the frequencies and the voltages precisely. In various ways and combinations, these electrical potentials of the brain can be picked up over many different brain areas each of which have proper names you are also supposed to know. You Cohen, you may be weird, and I'm beginning to think you probably are. I am definitely weird. The world, in my opinion, is inarguably also a very weird thing. But an EEG, Cohen, is just what it is. It is the specifically describable record of electrocortical activity. By no reasonable criterion that I know of can it be called weird!"

"C'mon boss. Take a look at it."

Cohen grabbed the tracing from off the technician's desk and put it before the electroencephalographer, who at first took his ruler and double checked the calibrations. They were OK. Only after that did he begin, first slowly, then quickly, to flip the folded pages. At times he would pause to study a particular page. But in less than two minutes his examination was concluded. Cohen pressed him as soon as the last page was turned down and the record was over again on its backside. The face sheet, captioned "Mary O'Neil," was being tapped upon pensively by the electroencephalographer's extended index finger.

"Well, what do you think?"

The electroencephalographer looked at him approvingly as if to suggest Cohen had gotten his good name back.

"Cohen, I apologize. You're a fucking genius."

"And?"

"You're right. It's weird. Very, very weird."

With Doctor Cohen looking over his shoulder, the electroencephalographer, not patiently but at least deliberately, so as to educate the younger man, demonstrated the pertinent findings. Considering all of his prior instruction, Cohen should have been able to describe exactly what he had observed rather than just express himself in exclamation points. The electroencephalographer pointed out that whereas most drug reactions, if associated with electroencephalographic changes, produce generalized variable slow or high frequency wave forms, the tracing of Mary O'Neil was characterized by high voltage spike and wave activity coming from the most forward brain areas, the very tips of her frontal lobes. The electroencephalographer had never seen such activity confined only to those areas much less would have suspected it to be drug based. It was also remarkable that the frequency of the activity was eight cycles per second. He had never known that type of wave form, the spike and wave configuration, to operate at such a frequency. And then, the abnormality did not come and go, which would be the usual. It was steady, continuous. The electroencephalographer went on to comment that not only was the tracing unique in his experience, but further more, he had never read of such an electroencephalographic phenomenon being reported in the scientific literature. He became very curious regarding the patient.

"Did you do a base line tracing before starting her on this so-called drug?"

"Sure. You read it yourself. It was normal. What do you take me for, some kind of amateur?"

"Doctor Cohen, I don't want you, so I'm surely not desirous of taking you ... for anything! But since you're now such a big deal clinical expert, what exactly are your plans for the dolorous lady?"

Cohen had always been irrepressible, even before he'd defensively thickened up skinwise by dint of exposure to the electroencephalographer's brand of sarcasm. So he matter-of-factly rolled on.

"Well, first off, I stopped the drug this morning. The EEG was too scary for me." The electroencephalographer raised eyes and eyebrows to ceiling. "I mean disconcertingly novel, and besides after a week on it, all the woman did was cry like hell, so what good could come of sticking with it?"

"And?"

"And what, sir?"

"What? What do you intend to do next? That's what!"

"I don't get it."

"That's not just one of your problems, Cohen. It's the whole problem! You don't seem ever to get it, to catch on to what is known as the scientific method! Jesus Christ, does this have to be like pulling teeth each damn time you and I get together?"

Cohen squinted at him.

"You shouldn't take the name of your lord in vain!"

"Don't try to get cute with me, Cohen. Just remember Christ was your blood brother, not mine, and I doubt very much he gives a fig about lording it over the likes of me! OK. So, where were we? Right! Did it ever occur to you it would be very important to repeat the EEG once she's taken off the medication?"

"Not really."

"Maybe someday, Cohen, if you should ever again happen to crack a book, you will stumble upon the fact that things only suggested, if not proven, are not very reliable or acceptable. And part of the scientific burden of proof involves bringing matters back to normalcy, in this case the brain waves, by withdrawing from experimental subjects those influences which, having been introduced, seem to have put things out of kilter. Get it?"

"OK."

It was as the meekness of certain exhausted lambs having been led to their inevitable slaughter.

"Also, doctor, please let us try not to forget, now that you have given the patient this experimental poison, it is of more than just passing scientific interest to see, having stopped the drug, if her EEG will revert to normal."

"You mean it may have produced some kind of permanent damage?"

"Congratulations! My faith in the educational process is restored and my efforts in your behalf are to be rewarded! Of course such an event is unlikely, but still it has to be considered, particularly because of the unprecedented nature of the EEG findings."

Through all of this, the electroencephalographer would nevertheless glance from time to time at the French travel poster, look at his watch, think about his loving flight attendant somewhere in France or hopefully on her way back to New York, and have intermittent pangs of hollowness of his calves by each surfacing recollection of her sweet face. It would soon be time again to dial that number. But there was something in this Mary O'Neil business competing for the attention he would much prefer directing to the matter of his Edna. Though operating simultaneously on these two quite different levels, he managed anyway to come up with another question for Doctor Cohen.

"This poison of yours actually been used before?"

"I wish you would stop calling it a poison."

"They never are poisons, are they? Or at least not until we wise up and see what they can do to people! Before then, they're experimental new drugs, right? And if just a few patients get real sick or conk out, then they're still only new drugs but ones with adverse reactions. Isn't that the way? How many people have to get hurt or knocked off before they're considered poisons? Is there a magic number? You got some kind of formula? Or should it be the number of tissue cells they get a strangle hold on? I'll wager you there are lots of cells in Mary O'Neil's brain either crying or getting ready to cry uncle. Is there a scientific distinction for poisons, excusing those which only kill certain or particular numbers of cells but incriminating those which knock off people as a whole? Or do poisons which start out as drugs never get to be called poisons whatever their consequence?"

"You sure have a different way of looking at things."

"Flattered you think so. Mind answering the original question?"

"Right. Well, she's the first one to get the drug. It's part of an FDA approved open label study for this and some other new psychoactive stuff from Biochemistry that's been OK'd at least in animals. We're the only study center approved for an initial trial in patients. That's about all I know. So now we've stopped it and like you want, we'll follow up with a repeat EEG. The chief will probably tell us to wait and see what happens before we use any of the other new drugs Biochem sent over in the same batch."

"Mind if I take a look at Edna?"

"Who's that?"

"Sorry, Mary."

"Not at all. I'll show her to you right now if you like. I'm heading back over. Got rounds to make on the same ward."

It took a special key to gain entry. Mary O'Neil was on the locked ward. The electroencephalographer hadn't been there in years. He remembered how he could never get over the apprehension of having a series of doors being locked behind him. One never knew, he would always think, when that key might just get misplaced or thrown away.

Doctor Cohen led him to the foot of the patient's bed. Mary was in a rolled up position. Middle aged, and pre maturely grayed, she had cheeks of a surprisingly robust color for a woman supposed to be out of sorts. What was really striking about her, though, were two other things. For one, she seemed not to appear really depressed. There was a wan but pleasant expression to her and to her gaze, though actually she didn't seem to have a gaze. She wasn't looking at anything. She simply stared out aimlessly into some beyond and it was not possible to engage her eyes. They focussed on nothing, evading awareness of anything placed before them. In fact, the electroencephalographer, by neither hand wavings nor the aiming of his pocket flash light, could draw her attention. He had the impression her concerns were quite elsewhere, but nevertheless they existed and profoundly so. Were they, he was tempted to think, for something universal? And then there was that other particular needing to be observed. It could possibly be overlooked, or discounted as a feature to be taken for granted in such a depressed patient, as it had been by Doctor Cohen. There were small tears streaming down almost continuously across her cheeks and chin and drop ping on to the bed sheets. As they welled relentlessly over her lower eyelids, they also tended to pool back enough into the palpebral fissures to bring the conjunctivae to a glistening shimmer. The look of this Mary was formidable, and also that quickly, suggestively significant and mean-ingful for the electroencephalographer.

"Thank you very much, Doctor Cohen. If you let me out now I'll be on my way and leave you to your rounds. I know how busy you must be. By the way, did she always cry like that?"

"Well, OK sir. Tomorrow I'll have her down, just like you want, for the repeat EEG. The tears? To tell the truth, I never noticed exactly when they began."

There was no point in airing his thoughts about Mary with Cohen, because what were they about? He supposed it would have possibly been interesting, maybe even use-ful, for the well-meaning but scatter-brained resident to hear that he suspected HR335 was inciting those tears. But he just didn't feel at that moment like getting into long discussions, or worse, arguments, over the pharmacology, the neuroanatomy, or the purposes of lachrymation. His other reflection on Mary was of a personal and ethereal nature, and certainly not apt to be appreciated by a fellow of Cohen's limited sensitivity. It was in regard to what people incline to call the mysterious. Mary reminded the electroencephalographer of all those statues of the Virgin round the world, and particularly the ones in Ireland, those other Marys, sworn by the faithful to weep occasionally. To weep, by one notion, over mankind's fallen condition.

And besides, it was time again to call the New York number

Seventeen

He had dialed from his private office next to the lab and on the third ring a woman answered.

"Gwen?"

"You that nutty doctor down in Washington?"

"She told you about me?"

"Charged through here yesterday morning with no time but to grab her gear and didn't shut up about her crazy mister DC for one second. So I guess I should know something about you!"

As long as Edna was the one to render it, he was prepared to accept any characterization of him that pleased her. Besides, "nut" was just about right anyway. Beyond that, he would try to be for her whatever she might fancy, and he felt he could manage almost anything she'd want, so high did his spirits soar now that he knew his fears of deception were totally unfounded. Moreover, to hear she cared enough to blab about him to the roommate, and in the fashion she obviously had, was enough to bring him much more than an enormous sense of relief. The electroencephalographer was remembering what it meant to be euphoric. It was like being up on the Regis Roof again and dancing.

"She really likes me, does she?"

"You don't know that? Now I understand what she says about you being a ... "

"Nut ... and old enough to be ... "

"Her father. So you see she just about said everything."

"Listen Gwen, I'm busting to know when she's getting back."

"She didn't tell you?"

"Tell me what?"

"She had time coming and set up a layover in France."

"For how long?"

"I think it's a week."

"Damn! You have a number for her over there?"

"Not really. I guess she didn't expect you'd be wetting your pants over it."

"I'm crazy about her!"

He couldn't help himself from shouting it though Gwen was a total stranger.

"Join the crowd!"

"Thanks a lot!"

"C'mon, relax. The way I see it, right now you've got the inside track."

"You going to be there to check with?"

"Sure, old darling. I'm no fly girl like Edna. Just a hard working model."

"Like for that guy she was out with Saturday, when I came along?"

"Well, just rarely. He's kind of hard to take. And you want to know something else? I've never even met you but I'm glad she made the switch."

"You're making me feel a helluva lot better. I'll give you my number. She doesn't have it. Please have her call me when she's back. If I'm not around, there's a tape running."

"And if your old lady answers?"

"I guess you do know everything, don't you? It's my office phone. After six o'clock the calls get taped or picked up on and passed through to my cellular, which I keep with me. Got it?"

"OK, old thing. Guess we'll manage. Sounds complicated though. Sure you're not with the CIA?"

Now the electroencephalographer could manage his first smile since separating from Edna.

"Hardly. I'm just an inspired, like you say, old thing. Take care."

"All right. I've got it down for her to read soon as she walks in the door. So long tiger."

It was an unanticipated circumstance. He had been so wrapped up in his concerns for not ever being able to catch up with Edna, he had given no thought at all to what he might do, if and when he should actually manage it. But with their reunion now a likelihood, even though at least a week away, the electroencephalographer was at once confronted with questions as to how this relationship was to be continued and what were his expectations for it. He had no doubts of his need for it to go on. After all, the young woman had banished his fears of being dead. His only care since New York, and until just now getting hold of her roommate, had been for losing her and to slip back into his old ways. Also, how could he ever forget she had aroused in him pleasures he had never thought himself capable of, and exhilaration of incomparable intensity. No doubt about it, his usually methodical approach to things had to be recruited immediately for reordering his life to accommodate this new and urgent priority. While weighing the matter, he remained in his office, feet atop his desk, the image of Edna coming and going, in laughter, in mock or real protest, sometimes head on, and perhaps at her best, in profile.

He had forgotten that it was one-thirty and that he had missed a customary downtown appointment. The phone would provide a rude reminder.

"You forget about me? Or is it about us?"

It was the nurse who worked at night and on weekends.

"Hey, bird! Sorry. Got kind of tied up. How you doing?"

"Doing? I've been waiting on you. That's how I'm doing, if you must know. What do you mean tied up?"

"There was an important tracing to discuss with the resident and then I had to go and see the patient."

"You know that's bullshit! I know it's bullshit! So why do we have to hear it? I'm just out of your thoughts, aren't I? I was on to it the second you walked out of here on Friday. I had a hunch something was up. It's about my faith in God, isn't it?"

As a matter of fact, the electroencephalographer hadn't been thinking much at all about the bird, but it had nothing to do with her being religious. At first it was because of his concerns about Jean, and then, for being bowled over by Edna. Nevertheless, there was no need to look askance at the favor of what he considered her most providential premonition. It would provide him opportunity to turn this clairvoyance of hers to what was now his pressing new purpose. The deck had to be cleared for Edna. There was certainly no possibility of having any kind of simultaneous dalliance with someone else. It was not in his nature. Nor was Edna the only reason to end his relationship with the bird. Her increasingly strident urging to find God had, in fact, finally made for more annoyance than their intimacy was bringing comfort. He'd seize upon her intuition about an impending reckoning, along with her presently irate condition, to make the parting more her making than his. That way, the outcome would be less sticky for both of them.

"Look, I don't give the religion thing much thought at all. It's only a bother when we're in bed and you start up on it. That can be a real drag."

"But we're never alone. Why can't you understand that? He's always there too. If only I could make you see it." It was going to be hook, line, and sinker.

"It's no fun to always have someone looking over my backside."

"Don't be vulgar! Worse, sacrilegious!"

"Look, how about, just for once, leaving Him out of our deal? You can talk to Him later when you're in church. But scoot Him out of there right now and even though I'm pushed for time, I'll head on over."

"Forget it! No way!"

The magic words. Maybe just one more little push. "Why can't I have you all to myself, just for once?"

"Because He's not only with us, He's in me, in us, in all of us."

"If that's so, as long as He's so damned handy, I can't

imagine why you don't jolly well let Him do all the screwing too! What in hell do you want me or anyone else for?"

"You bastard! I don't need this! And if that's how you think, I don't need you either! From now on, just buzz off, mister!"

She slammed the phone. He'd thought, at first sound of her voice, about possibly coming to an amicable understanding somewhere, and soon, perhaps over lunch at a nice restaurant. But this was a better way to end what should never have been started.

Eighteen

His newly gained optimism, since talking to Gwen, had forestalled the electroencephalographer from resuming his doleful way of regarding all matters. The change in his demeanor was obvious to anyone who knew him. He was also unusually deliberate and pensive while interpreting the EEG tracings, whereas before he would flip through them impatiently, often irritably, at speed. He could even be of disarmingly good cheer when confronted by professional chores he'd always held bothersome, like answering dumb questions, or responding to requests for consultation he deemed not really necessary. Nothing seemed to irk him now. Quite a marvel for a man with a reputation for a consistently acerbic and confrontational way of dealing with his colleagues! Of course, all of this was possible only because, actually, he scarcely noticed what went on around him. He could take advantage of his ability to function just about by rote in these technical circumstances, for even in their minutiae, long before now they had become mere second nature to him. Having resorted to this quite feasible slippage into what was an automatic mode for dealing with mundane workaday needs, he idled his way through the passing hours, appearing to be at work, but for the most part being secretly contemplative of nothing more than the image of his be loved flight attendant and their prospective reunion.

At home, his wife seemed not her usual ebullient self, but if she had noticed any change in him, she said nothing about it. At first the electroencephalographer simply thought it remarkable for her not to have picked up on his uncontrollable tendency now to sit and stare, feigning attentiveness to books and journals yet always having them cracked open to the very same pages, the while he hovered over them through long vacancies of time. Asked on one occasion what a television program he was mooning through happened to be all about, not even the vagueness of his response had seemed to clue her that his thoughts were distantly elsewhere. At work, this change was considered long overdue by all those having had to deal with his laconic, sometimes nasty manner. Unlikely, therefore, that anything but sighs of relief and sporadic eye rolling would come of his new conduct. But at home his lapses of attention and mental wanderings should have aroused his wife's concern, and yet they did not do so. His chance finding that vodka bottles in the liquor cabinet were suffering slow but sure droppage of level gave him better understanding of what was going on. She had switched from wine to something stronger. This could be serious, an ominous portent that her future course might very well be as it had been for both her mother and her father. The issue of counseling and treatment, always adamantly rejected by her, would have to be raised once more, but not too quickly or right now. He hadn't present inclination to embroil himself in that sort of unpleasantness. The best start, anyway, would be to approach the problem obliquely.

"I notice we're running out of vodka. Should I bring some home?"

And he let it go at that.

Two days later Doctor Cohen was on him again. "Here you are, hot off the press!"

It was Mary O'Neil's repeat tracing. She had been off the drug forty-eight hours. The electroencephalographer studied it carefully. For at least that brief interval Edna was out of mind.

"It's quite normal. Congratulations. You've saved her!"

"C'mon boss. What do you think?"

"About what?"

"Was all that electrical haywire due to the drug?"

"Most likely. I sure wouldn't give it to someone else just to prove it definitively!"

"No way! We're looking to help people, not rock their boats. The chief said to just let her sit tight for awhile. See what she does on her own. Maybe her depression is a cyclic situation."

"What about those tears?"

"Well that was part of the chief's reasoning. All of a sudden, she gave up on all that crying. He thought it could be the sign she was starting to snap out of it. What do you think?"

'I'm no psychiatrist, just a neurologist turned easy rider of the brain waves."

Neither the foolhardy young resident nor his chief seemed to have considered what was spectacularly and startlingly obvious to the electroencephalographer. Mary O'Neil hadn't stopped crying because of any spontaneous improvement. It had been the experimental drug HR335 that had brought on her tears in the first place. No longer receiving it, she had simply ceased to cry!

"Yeah, well still, there's a lot I need to learn from you, boss. Someday all this stuff is going to come together, the brain waves, the anatomy, the chemistry, the thought processes, and the emotional disorders. When that great day comes, you and I will find ourselves working side by side!" His old ways were not so overwhelmed by the lovesick business that the electroencephalographer did not rise to the threat of Cohen's premise and feel as resentful as it was possible to be for the approach of any such deplorable day. Besides which, he detested Cohen's persistence in calling him "boss." He'd have his own say as to whom he would or would not choose to have under his wing. But now he was oddly inspired to concentrate on this unusual business of the drug, its action, and its linkage with the tears. To do that he needed to rid himself both of Cohen and of the turbulence generally surrounding that young man. Such prospect, in contrast to the ugly one of their destiny to someday work together, he found not at all unattractive.

"Well Doctor Cohen, we both do have our duties, don't

we? Good luck with your interesting patient. Heading on back to the ward now?"

"Not actually. I have to go over to Biochemistry and turn back the stuff we had her on."

It happened so fast the electroencephalographer could not possibly divine the exact genesis of his next and almost instantaneous utterance. It was, like all brainstorms (a very apt connotation), a complete enigma when he mouthed it. "You needn't bother really. I've got a meeting near Biochem in about ten minutes. Glad to tote it over for you.

Just tell me who gets it."

"Gee, if you don't mind. Sally in Fryberg's lab."

"Right you are, no problem."

Cohen handed over a small bottle containing several hundred tablets of the "stuff."

"Much obliged. Thanks again."

Cohen was gone and the electroencephalographer was left to himself, palming the bottle of HR335 and only a short while later, still half wondering, but also half know ing his purpose in this sudden and neat bit of chicanery. He did not, however, have to think the matter entirely through right then and there. He did not have to know some ultimate or precise intent, whatever that might prove to be, in order to formulate a logical next step. Searching through a storage cabinet, he located a bottle of similar but unmarked tablets, left over from prior experimental use as placebos. They were of almost the same size and shape. He carefully substituted the two hundred and three of them for two hundred and three of HR335. Then he ambled across the street to Biochem and turned in the tampered bottle. As for what he would consider doing next in this regard, he did have by now a growing inkling. In spite of his fear of being dead, and of many other things as well, he could be tempted into taking unnecessary risks. If at last he knew exactly how it felt to be in love, he still hadn't any idea at all of what it was like to cry. But he had hit upon an intriguing if uncharted way to find that out.

The experience of loving, as it affected him now, had come as a surprise. True, he had cared for his wife in one fashion, and had also been through a certain number of sexual involvements, as part of others. However, he had never been inclined to seek, much less expect, the kinds of excitedness and physical urgency he'd heard it said by others could come of affectionate relationships based upon infatuation. He always suspected, rather, that the hyper bole of romance was adolescent puffery and drew its popular appeal from an exploitative commercial hard-sell. So now, to be the head and heart tumbled victim of just that phenomenon, had come as quite a shock. But the resulting vertigo had not managed to deny him any of the bliss of this new and unanticipated delight.

He was, however, a person long addicted to rigid ways of thinking along most lines. Only some of that could be supplanted or displaced by the pleasures and demands of his newly provoked libido. As wonderful as it was to be so impassioned, and however rich and timely this new emotion might seem, still the love of Edna amounted to but a brief recent intrusion, and could not exclude entirely his abiding curiosity about certain matters long rooted by years of self-questioning. The issue, for example, of why he could never resort to tears, and what the act of crying might actually accomplish, was a question that could never fail to fascinate him and to lay heavy claim to his attention. Now, amazingly and unexpectedly, he was toting the possible answer to that question, as well as the solution to his own inadequacy of that sort, in his left jacket pocket. It was enough, once more, to have him looking about and over his shoulder. The electroencephalographer was too doubting and suspicious, of almost everything, to even consider the possibility that a pair of happenings, such as that of Edna and HR335 might occur just by chance. How could both being in love and the prospective acquisition of the ability to cry be only coincidences in the life of a person fated previously to do nothing but contemplate his own death? Was not some kind of string being pulled?

Of course, tears were not mere lachrymation. He knew they were connected with grieving or personal loss. Some how the act of their shedding was associated with the amelioration of emotional distress. Tears were part and parcel of what the psychiatrists called catharsis, although they hadn't the faintest idea of how that process was carried off. This, in spite of recent writings in psychiatric journals that people who cried less were more susceptible to asthma and stomach ulcers. Writings also that there were reasons to suspect the thrymal glands managed to rid the body of depressant chemicals by extracting them from the blood stream and eliminating them in tears, which made people feel better. But it was the neuronal mechanism for the phenomenon of crying that mostly drew the electroencephalographer's interest. How and why was it all brought about? And of course, how was he himself defectively assembled so as to hinder its workings?

Crying was to him an entirely strange bit of human conduct because tears also had their habit of appearing during the most intense sorts of laughter, and when people managed to have an extremity of happiness. They seemed also to pop out during religious conversions, whatever that might connote. Should the eye be exposed to any kind of irritation, tears flowed to comfort the inflamed ocular sur face. And then there were the patients he'd seen with mul tiple sclerosis or brain tumors who denied that when they cried they were having any feelings at all! It was called pathological emotionality by doctors, whose patients might rather consider it to be a blessing. No doubt about it, he knew that tears and the intricate mechanisms for their pro duction, were designed for working many kinds of practi cal benefit, as well as being, for some who were religious, handmaidens to the working of miracles. All of this, even its loony aspects, was a tantalizing area for investigation.

The problem, still, was that he had never cried. Pos session of HR335 might solve that, but such an experiment would have to go on hold for the time being. For the sake of his precarious emotional stability, and in the interest of his new self indulgence in pleasures to be drawn from the condition of loving contemplation, he could not hazard the immediate sampling of any bit of HR335.

Three o'clock the next afternoon, Richard called. "She's gone. Jean's gone."

"Oh God! God damn!"

The carcass of that squirrel dead in the roadway on Fifth Avenue sprang to the electroencephalographer's mind and then became lodged in his throat. It was difficult for him to speak. Perhaps also difficult for him to breathe. He saw, instantly, the face of a dead Jean. It was bloated and a sickly green. Her eyes were stuck half opened, searching out, imploring a world lost to her, a world she loved so intensively, but could no longer see, to return.

"What the hell happened?"

"That's about the right word for it. She went through the x-ray treatment all in one day and without a hitch. She didn't so much as turn a hair. That was Monday. We got back here to New York without any problem. Tuesday night she was just taking it easy in the apartment. You know something, she was in very good spirits! She had the feeling she'd at least gotten the upper hand on what was growing in her brain. You know how she put things."

"Sure."

"Then all of a sudden this morning she grabbed for her chest, complained of pain, and said she couldn't breathe. The ambulance was here in minutes but nothing seemed to help, to work. By the time we were in the hospital she was just coming apart. She was bleeding and clotting all at once, in and out of shock, blue around the mouth. Then just like that, with never a word for me, she was gone. Look, friend, don't try to say anything at all right now. I just wanted you to know. I'm gonna get back to my crying."

"You got someone with you?"

"Not yet. But her son is on the way from downtown."

"Sorry Richard. Terribly sorry."

The electroencephalographer felt more stunned and deprived than saddened. Death had sneaked back. Death had come and gone, robbing him of his valued friend. Never would they swap confidences again, exchange the thoughts kept private from everybody else. There was also awe for being himself still alive and aware of everything, while Jean lay on a slab, drained of life. He could imagine her favorite books scattered about in the apartment, never to be opened by her again. Dresses would hang limp in a closet, not disturbed until rudely discarded. What right, anyway, did any of these things have to go on without her? And the radio guys she liked to laugh along with each morning would still put out their yarns and off color jokes, ignorant that a once vibrant and raucous listener had been stilled forever. Her ears, her brain, were now deaf to them. Jean had become an unknowing corpse, cast into the infinitude.

He reached for the bottle of HR335 then quickly put it aside again, securing it in his desk drawer. He had changed his mind. To cry was no solution for how he felt or what he was thinking. He had already realized, anyway, that the trial of losing Jean was not so much emotional. Its essential threat was differently posed. Death was back and waiting. Besides which, that earlier anticipation of her passing had altered his eventual response to it. In his albeit limited way of prefiguring this catastrophe, and what his reaction to it might be, he'd somehow managed to blunt its cutting edge. Consequently, these next few hours needed not so much to be felt as mulled through.

Sitting there in his office, he began at first idly, then deliberately, to recall the face, the figure, the voice of a Jean alive, in an effort to counter these new imagined images of her dead. No good. Death, with all of its person ally oriented implications had insinuated itself back into focus. Feelings for Edna had gotten him past those gloomy obsessions. But now they were returning. He must do something before all of the old gnawings and wrenchings were also re-recruited. Instinctively, he seemed next to punch in a kind of internal key. Slowly Edna's image took shape and substituted for that of his dead friend. It helped. There was a slight buoyancy within him.. Yet still, there was also this ominous sense of renewed susceptibility to that old kind of drifting. He punched another key. He could recall the smell of Edna, and yes, perhaps the feel of her tongue. He had to do more. The spoiler in him must be countered. A contact, any contact with Edna might help. The electroencephalographer grabbed for his phone and dialed the New York number. Just to hear a ring at her usual location was something. Just reaching out to where she ordinarily slept and lived seemed to raise his spirits, stave off the other thing, even though he had no reason at all to expect she had returned. The roommate Gwen was there.

"Hello?"

"Hey Gwen. Any word?"

"You're really something, D.C. No, not even a post card. Besides it's only three days. Even if she did write, it's too soon to get anything. And like I said, I don't really expect to hear a word until she walks in the door."

This helped also. No more than the wishful picture of Edna walking back in, entering an apartment he'd never seen, could make him feel better.

"Hell, suppose TWA needed her back sooner, wouldn't they have some way of reaching her?"

"Hey man, I'm a model, not an airline exec! And remember, she's on vacation, probably driving herself around somewhere out in the boondocks. If I know Edna, she's not gonna be anywhere it's easy to call her back. She's been counting on this leave too damned long for that."

"I just thought it'd be nice to get her on the phone."

"DC, you'll have to hold your water until she's back. 'Bye now."

In its limited way it was working. Even to be occupied without result in reaching out to Edna made him feel he might hold his own against the spoiler.

What else was there to do? Busywork, any kind of busywork. Now, in the late afternoon, there were reports he could get out, reports he'd put off working on, annual summaries of the lab activities. After all, arranging to survive should involve some kind of effort, work. And the work of simply staying abreast was inherently self sustaining by a prodding tag-along optimism. So, he'd tap into it to stay afloat. Thus, he could save himself by laboring over almost anything, even something mindless. But better still would be work that drew his interest. What might that be? It didn't take long to think of concentrating his attention on Mary O'Neil. That's what he would do! Getting out all of those dumb past-due reports was not as good as revisiting Mary O'Neil.

Having checked his identification tag, the orderly admitted him to the locked ward. The electroencephalographer was glad to see that Cohen was nowhere around and so he'd be able to seek her out, without interference. Mary appeared different. She looked directly, intently, and inquiringly, straight at him. The faint pleasantness and the tears were both gone. The electroencephalographer was the first to speak.

"Do you remember me?"

"Yes, you were here the other day with the young doctor."

"I'm not young?"

"Well, not like him."

"What's been happening since then?"

"Quite a lot. I seem to be coming out of it. They say I'm doing it on my own, praise God. And as you see, I'm able to talk again."

"Tell me, when I was here last, you weren't speaking. But do you remember how you were feeling at that time?"

"Why sure. I was starting to feel much better. Actually so good I was crying over it."

"You do remember that?"

"Doctor, how could anyone forget something like that?"

The electroencephalographer thanked the patient for this information and left the ward.

He returned to his desk wondering whether or not to enter into the office computer a report of what had transpired in the case of Mary O'Neil. It needed to include the electroencephalograms before, during, and after HR335, plus his observation of her tearing and half smiles, as well as a claim of drug effectiveness based upon her own subjective awareness of mood elevating amelioration of the melancholia. But how would the profession regard his attachment of significance to results obtained in but a single case? He could well anticipate they'd say it had no statistical or medical value. Proof would rest, to their thinking, on a successful testing of HR335 in many patients, including a double blind trial, some patients getting placebo tablets like those now in the tampered bottle and others receiving HR335. Still, shouldn't he make at least some record of his observations?

His tentative inclination to do it quickly dissipated. He knew very well those pompous asses at Psychiatry! They'd ridicule his notion, suggest he was out of his depth, and scoff at the possibility of any effect of new remedy for a psychiatric ailment coming from a mere neurologist, much less one turned cranky electroencephalographer! These were doctors notoriously resistant to any new therapy conceived in quarters other than their own. So he merely sat there bemused by his speculations on this discovery. But also happening to almost revel in the fact that the entire business was a very effective distraction, diverting his attention once again from thoughts of being dead. Images of Jean's corpse and of his wife's boozing were, in part, staved off. And Edna, of course, was simply on vacation. He was coping!

The more he considered it, the more he liked the idea of pills for crying, and much more than for the therapeutic boon it promised to be for depressed patients.

Of course on the strictly medical side of things, it seemed to make a lot of sense to take HR335, have one or two really good prolonged cries, enough to feel somewhat better for it, and then get on with one's proper business. With the medications that psychiatric patients were being put on these days, they could pretty much look forward to a lifetime of being doped up, and there was no telling what the ultimate toxic effects of all their everlasting poisoning might be.

But for the electroencephalographer, there was a kind of symbolic aspect to his contemplated treatment of depression which he found especially appealing. Life, as he had always thought of it, was by its very nature a thoroughly lamentable proposition. What more appropriate then, but to cry oneself free of its emotional downturns? Beyond the tearful face of Mary O'Neil under treatment with HR335 he could see all of those weeping statues of the Virgin. If stone could be that moved to cry for all of mankind, then why not see what we ourselves might accomplish along the same lines, in the interest of those of us either not able to cry, or not quite competent to cry enough or in the right way, to ease the pain of this passage? After all, people were always saying, "There's nothing like a good cry!" Was not HR335 the answer?

All these things considered, it was an entirely fascinating enterprise, but like most of what he did and thought, which the electroencephalographer was keeping strictly to himself.

Nineteen

For the next two days he resumed his vacillation over the question of discussing his findings with a colleague.

He was prepared to concede that it might be at least interesting to raise the subject with one of the psychiatrists, if for nothing more than to provoke a discussion aimed at his own edification. For example, he'd like to know just what percentage of depressed patients did cry, and how often, and whether or not they got anything out of it, and whether those who cried had less or more severe depressions than those who didn't. There were so many things that he did not know. But finally he put aside again the possibility of airing either his observations or his uncertainties. It was unlikely the psychiatrists he knew could tell him anything useful. Since they themselves seemed never to ask any pro vocative or interesting questions, how could they conceivably have learned enough to answer his? More than likely he'd just get the kind of response he'd already had from Doctor Cohen, the embryo version of his elders, that same old "You know, I never noticed that sort of thing." Nevertheless, he kept his mind fairly glued, whatever else he might be doing, to the intriguing phenomenon he had witnessed and to wondering how possibly to move it from the realm of mere hypothesis into that of scientific proof.

Beyond the clinical fascination this matter held for him also lay that same persistent very practical consideration. Until Edna was back in New York it could be nothing but brinkmanship for him now. All he had to prevent him from becoming once more his customary gloomy self, were these consuming questions regarding HR335.

The death of his friend Jean was not the only matter to weigh upon him the rest of the week. His wife was becoming almost inaudible and invisible. Since his pointed observation of the dwindling vodka reserves, she had avoided him. Also, her usual good cheer had evaporated. The deterioration of her purposeful and upbeat personality had cast a pall over the electroencephalographer's house hold. Even their dog seemed to sense and to be affected by it. When called, he took to slinking rather than bounding, and showed a mournful cast of eye.

The electroencephalographer, unable to tell at first just how much alcohol was being taken, could not distinguish the change in his wife's manner that might be due to her addiction from what might possibly be related to some other condition. When at last he found three empty bottles hidden away in the cellar, he finally got down to pleading with her to consider seriously and urgently almost any kind of medical consultation. His wife became enraged and stormed from the room, declaring that if anybody needed to seek medical or psychiatric help it was he, adding as a final rejoinder that he should take that as an opinion from someone made expert through twenty years of being around him! To call after her that he would wholeheartedly agree to a family kind of consultation, a dual enterprise for the two of them, did not alter her adamant stance.

It was becoming more and more difficult to feel assured of anything but uncertainty and impermanence. Edna could not be reached. His wife was failing the way both her mother and her father had before her. HR335, along with what it either promised or implied, for all he might speculate about it, was in limbo. If life was a miracle, it was a quite worthless one, save for Edna.

Then he began to become increasingly and disturbingly aware of the homeless people. It was hard not to notice them. They were everywhere. On street corners, in store doorways and building entranceways, sprawled across the warm exhaust gratings of the Metro underground tunnels. And when he passed nearby, without exception, there seemed always to be from them a special kind of glance or sustained gaze in his direction. Even if their look was brief, it was consistently fierce in its appeal. He found himself embarrassed and unhinged by their silent, determined, imploring. These people also seemed to harbor something he could not quite fathom.

The result was that he, a lifetime self-centered person, only the week before in New York reminded of it, found himself reaching out to help the street people.

He began to load up his pockets with coins and his wallet with singles and fives. With each charitable approach that he made to these unfortunate men and women he experienced a profound feeling, queerly enough a mix of sadness and warmth, as he handed over his donations. On one occasion, in fact the very first and it being also the circumstance which motivated him to continue, he offered only a single quarter, but the gaze of the man who received it to was disorienting, hallucinogenic. Someone else, a third sort of person seemed abruptly present, a shadowy figure, an intensely friendly, mild mannered, approving and affectionate specter. And when he asked himself what the devil was going on, those quizzical words as he heard them internally register, were pitched as in the recurrent, ancient, musical way. Could he, after all, just be hearing sounds of past millennia, sounds of some distant human or other experience, hidden away in his very genes? And what could possibly need accompaniment or celebration by this kind of music? But most of all, he wondered at that same time, why did he have the clear sense of being on the very edge of tears, tears veritably straining once again to be released? But that was, of course, not possible.

Twenty

It was late Friday afternoon. The electroencephalographer was interpreting a tracing and comparing it to one completed a month before in the case of a patient who had undergone surgery for removal of a brain tumor. This new tracing was worse, but that should not surprise anyone. So was the patient.

The last two days had been unusually busy in the lab, but now finally, he was caught up on his readings as well as on certain statistical reports that were long overdue. As soon as five o'clock came his department always emptied out, particularly as now, right before the weekend. So he was alone in his office when the phone rang.

It was Gwen. He could even guess it would be Gwen by the second ring, and before actually hearing her voice.

But when he did recognize that indeed it was she, he jumped at what may have been her first words, never really registering their substance.

"She called? You got a letter?"

"Look, I don't know if I can handle this."

"What's wrong?"

"Her father just called me."

"So?"

The electroencephalographer knew he really didn't want to hear anything more.

"The airline got a hold of him this afternoon!"

"C'mon Gwen! What's going on! What's happening!"

It was no longer a voice on the other end. It was a wail, and words that were not spoken, but sobbed out, sobbed to the point of being almost unintelligible, but clear enough still, to freeze his fingers and contract his bowel.

"She's dead! Edna's dead!"

"What the hell do you mean dead?"

"They say she was driving on the wrong side of the road. She got hit by a big truck. Oh God! She never even made it to the hospital!"

After that it didn't matter what was said, or shrieked, or sobbed, or choked over any further by Gwen. And no amount of better clarity for either the voice at the other end or the gruesome details could make for any difference. Edna and life were gone from him.

Almost immediately upon hanging up, a picture formed to assault him. Edna and he were being intimate again and she was venting her incredible laugh, at him, at the ceiling in the Park Lane, at eternity itself. With that, an intense nausea gripped him. He rushed into the toilet shivering, his trembling, ice cold hands grasping the edge of the bowl, while he retched and gagged out the sour con tents of his stomach in painfully cramping stages until there was nothing more to come. Then, unsteady and light-headed, he made his way back to his chair.

With forearms pressed against his thighs, he began to rock. He had never done this before. Possibly his genes were offering it up as they had the ancient music. What ever such movements may have done for other grieving humans, they gave him no comfort at all. He was rocking, wailing, but some thief had robbed him of what could come of those essentials. It gained him nothing.

"Then back to crying. Yes crying! Let's have another crack at that! Come now, tears!" a voice, his voice demanded. "I'm choking well enough to please the very devil! Well, let's cry for him also! Isn't that what he wants? So, let's strain for tears! Strain for them like for an orgasm that just won't come! Christ! God! If ever I needed tears, I need them now!"

No sign of anything happening.

"Well, fuck you! Fuck it all! Fuck everything! Fuck everything, forget everything, and know nothing! Know nothing! Nothing! Because it's all the same! Everything is the same! The real, the imagined, love, death, everything out of one thing and being one thing! It's no more than crap, crap for crying over and I'll show you how it's done, really done, done professionally by a guy like me, you bastard! And you can also save your God-damned heart welling charities and your guilt-ridden phony solicitudes for some other sucker!"

At that, the electroencephalographer reached for the bottle of HR335, extracted and then swallowed a single tablet. Breathing heavily, he sat and waited. Unknown to him, in about three minutes, the spike and wave complexes started up near the tips of his frontal lobes, the pre-motor regions of his brain. In another four minutes he was seeing Mary O'Neil as well as all of those crying statues of the Virgin.

It was then that he felt the first small drops running down his cheeks and got the taste of salt. Soon his eyes were so full of tears his vision was misted over.

"Thank God! Thank God! I'm crying!"

Also, and he hardly noticed it, he was sobbing and feeling better. In fact he began to feel quite good.

The spike wave complexes, however, were beginning to take a different course. They were diffusing, spreading out. In Mary O'Neil's brain they had stayed localized for days, confined right there to the tips of her frontal lobes. But the electroencephalographer's brain was different. In his brain, excitation was much more apt to spread. He had been aware his entire life, how different he was from other people. Even Edna had thought so but seemed, to his surprise, rather to love him for it. Peculiar that in regard to taking HR335 he happened not to consider this variable. As the excitation waves spread out, the electroencephalographer began to twitch. When the twitching became generalized he lost consciousness. Twitching was soon substituted for by spasms which produced total body stiffening. Rather violent convulsive movements of all four limbs were to follow and to eject him from his chair onto the floor where he lay face down, a victim of incessant seizure activity. Most convulsions stop quickly. Those produced by HR335 can go on for days in sensitive people such as the electroencephalographer. Lying face down, respirations compromised by the seizures, choking on his own secretions, he might not have lasted very long at all.

At around eleven he coughed, began to stir, attempted to rise up. Not possible. It was post convulsive fatigue to a point just short of paralysis. So he yielded to a deep sleep, one from which certain musical sounds very gradually receded, leaving him to awaken again at three in the morning. His mouth tasted foul, he had bitten his tongue, soiled his trousers. It seemed that every muscle ached profoundly. And yet there was this sense of an inspired expectancy and absolutely no thoughts intruding save what if he were to cut the dose of HR335, maybe just break a tablet in half?

And what if then he slipped it to his wife?

His right arm being limp, he used the left to cross himself.

That's how the electroencephalographer was taken.